Star's Storm:
Lords of Kassis Book 2

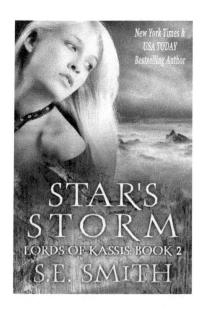

New York Times &
USA TODAY
Bestselling Author

STAR'S
STORM
LORDS OF KASSIS: BOOK 2
S.E. SMITH

By S.E. Smith

Acknowledgments
I would like to thank my husband Steve for believing in me and being proud enough of me to give me the courage to follow my dream. I would also like to give a special thank you to my sister and best friend Linda, who not only encouraged me to write but who also read the manuscript.
—S.E. Smith

Montana Publishing
Science Fiction Romance
STAR'S STORM
Copyright © 2013 by Susan E. Smith
First E-Book Published January 2013
Cover Design by Dara England/Melody Simmons

Summary: Star is falling in love with one of the aliens who kidnapped her and her circus family, but what it will take to make him see her as a partner, not a delicate treasure to be kept away somewhere safe?

ISBN: 978-1-942562-59-7 (paperback)
ISBN: 978-1-942562-21-4 (eBook)

Published in the United States by Montana Publishing.

{1. Science Fiction Romance – Fiction. 2. Science Fiction – Fiction. 3. Paranormal – Fiction. 4. Romance – Fiction.}

www.montanapublishinghouse.com

Synopsis

Star Strauss has always been a fighter. From the time she was born prematurely to her life on the road as a circus performer. She has never let her small stature keep her from achieving her dreams. She is one of the best aerial performers in the world. Her love of being up high and flying free has helped her overcome the challenges she faces when she is on the ground. Only her circus family, her sister, and her best friend have ever really understood her need for freedom. Her life changes when she finds herself on a distant world where every creature seems to tower over her.

Jazin Ja Kel Coradon is the third son of the ruling House of Kassis. He is known not only for his skills as a fierce warrior, but for his knowledge of communication, security, and weapons systems. This knowledge has increased the effectiveness of the Kassis defenses protecting their world from attack from a new group of rebels who threaten their very existence. He will fight until his last breath to protect his people.

His life changes when he meets a tiny creature who is unlike anything he has ever seen. She is petite, delicate, and beautiful. The problem is she is also the strongest, most stubborn female he has ever met. She refuses to do what he tells her, she defies him at every turn, and doesn't seem to understand that all he wants to do is protect her. If he could just get her to stay in the nice safe bubble he has created for her, his life would be so much simpler!

Star had enough of people back home trying to put her in a glass box, she wasn't about to let anyone on an alien world try to put her in one! When the man she loves is kidnapped, she will do what she does best. She will use her skills as a performer to rescue him from the men determined to extract the information they need to bring down the Kassis defense system before they kill him.

Sometimes being small has its advantages. The enemy never expects a pint-size female to have the strength of a warrior and a stubborn warrior is about to find out he has a partner who can stand tall with him in the face of danger.

Contents

Chapter 1

Star stared up at the glittering stars as a sense of peace settled over her. She was surprised. She thought dying would hurt but she didn't feel any pain at all anymore.

Her body was no longer trembling from the cold that had engulfed it only moments earlier. Now, she couldn't feel the shivers raging through her tiny body. She could hear her sister's tearful voice begging her to hang on. She could hear her best friend and surrogate sister, River, saying something in the background but none of it mattered any more. All that mattered was the sense of peace that was settling over her.

She stared up at the two moons in the dark sky. She frowned slightly. Why were there two of them? The Earth only had one moon. Her mind fought sluggishly to remember.

Oh yeah, Star remembered vaguely. *I'm not on Earth anymore. I'm on Kassis.*

The frown cleared only to be replaced with a feeling of deep sorrow as a name whispered across her mind… *Jazin.* The thought of leaving him caused a sharp pain to blossom inside her that had nothing to do with the injuries to her small body. A single tear escaped the corner of her eye and ran down until it fell into the soft blond hair fanning out around her.

She heard her sister's anguished cry as darkness descended around her. Star felt her heart stutter as though it was actually breaking for the love she was leaving behind. As if from a great distance, she faintly heard Jo's cry echo quietly through the night as her eyes slowly drifted closed.

"No! Damn it, Star!" Jo choked out as she desperately tried to stem the blood flowing from the wound to her little sister's side. "You hang on! You are a fighter! You will not give in, damn you! You will not leave me here alone!"

"Let me take her." A hissing voice suddenly whispered out of the darkness of the night. "She must be taken to medical immediately."

Jo turned her head to stare at the huge creature burying its sharp claws into the stone pillar she and Star was perched on. Madas Tal Mod was the mate of the Leader of the Tearnats, a reptilian alien species that had kidnapped her and Star. Jo gazed at the creature for a moment before she glanced down at her sister's pale, peaceful face. She looked back up at Madas with pleading eyes. Her voice, thick with tears, was barely above a whisper.

"Please, you have to help her," Jo begged, looking into the black eyes of the creature.

"Let me take her. She will survive," Madas Tal Mod replied in a soft hissing voice. "It is not time for the little warrior to leave our world yet."

Jo watched helplessly as Madas gently picked up Star's limp body and cradled it tightly against her. Madas used her powerful back legs and tail to help grip the pillar as she climbed back down it. She refused to believe the Gods would call this little warrior home to their world. There were still too many dangers that needed to be dealt with and the strength and heart of this tiny warrior from another world was still needed.

Madas jumped that last few feet to the ground making sure she cushioned the body held in her arms. She didn't wait to see if the other warrior followed. There wasn't enough time. Already she could hear the little warrior's heart struggle to beat. She moved rapidly through the dark gardens situated between the four Houses of Kassis. The battle tonight had taken quite a few lives, both enemy and allied. Madas was determined that the one in her arms would not be another.

She burst into the South House, hissing out for directions to medical. She was just about to turn when a savage roar echoed through the corridor leading from the gardens into the main hallway. Wild eyes met hers briefly before they dropped to the precious body in her arms.

"She needs help immediately," Madas said. "Lead, I will carry her. It is best not to move her any more than necessary. I hear her heart struggling."

Jazin stared grimly at the large Tearnat. Every fiber in him wanted to rip the small body out of her arms and into his but he knew she was right. Forcing himself to turn away, he roared for everyone to clear a path and took off at a run for the medical unit shouting into his link that he needed the healers to be prepared stat. He burst through the door just a millisecond before Madas. He watched as the healers, who had been waiting, quickly instructed Madas to lower Star's small figure onto the regenerative bed before they disappeared through another set of doors. He moved to follow them. He was stopped by Madas' large, claw-shaped hand that was gripping his forearm tightly.

Jazin swung around pulling his laser sword. "Let them care for her," the soft voice hissed in compassion. "You will only be in their way. Give them time to stabilize her before you go. Give yourself time to calm so you can be strong for her," Madas said looking down into Jazin's eyes.

Jazin swallowed several times trying to get control of his rage and fear. His eyes shifted to the doors and back to the huge Tearnat holding him. He knew she was right. He would not be of use to Star in the condition he was in. He would only get in the way. But… his eyes went back to the door.

"I cannot lose her," he said harshly.

"It is not her time yet," Madas said confidently. "Your little warrior has much to do still. This is simply a test by the Gods to see if she has the strength needed to face the battles still yet to come. She is strong. She will not fail such a simple challenge. Believe in her strength and you will find she is truly as much a warrior as you are. She will be a mate who can stand by your side, not in your shadow," Madas quietly hissed out.

Jazin looked at Madas and slowly lowered his blade. "I can only pray that you are right," he replied. "But, know this. If she survives, I will never let her be exposed to danger again. I will protect her and care for her even if I have to lock her away to do so. Never again will I let anyone hurt her. On this I swear," Jazin declared passionately.

Madas chuckled as she watched the fierce determination settle onto Jazin Ja Kel Coradon's face. "Be careful what you say, Lord Jazin. There are some forces in the universe you cannot control. And some of them come in very small packages."

Chapter 2

Star relaxed further down under the covers. She was having the most wonderful dream. She was flying through the air. Her dad was watching her, coaching her, laughing excitedly as she caught the bar he had swung out for her to catch. She could feel his and her mom's arms wrap tightly around her in excitement when she landed on the platform next to them.

The dream began to change. She wasn't a little girl any more. Walter, the manager of the circus, was introducing her, Jo, and River. She could feel the huge horse under her picking up speed as she entered the center ring. Tonight she was going to perform a new act. It was one of the most challenging she had ever done and the first time she was the star of the show.

Jo and River would back her up if she needed it, but she was confident she wouldn't have any problems. It had taken Walter to finally convince her parents that she could do this. Star was small for sixteen, barely reaching five feet in her bare feet. Even then, she towered over Walter's three and a half foot frame.

It was Walter who Star turned to when she became afraid she couldn't do something. He never gave her any sympathy. He pushed her to believe in herself and her natural talents. He made her feel as tall as any of the other performers.

The dream was changing again, pulling her away from her circus family. Colors swirled around her as if she was falling through the White Rabbit's hole only to end up in Oz. Bits and pieces of her life flashed through her mind in a kaleidoscope of images, sounds, and colors. It made her dizzy as they flitted through her mind.

Now she was at the condo she and Jo owned in Orlando. She was mad! She felt the overwhelming anger burning through her. She had heard a group of other performers, including the guy she was dating, making fun of her size. He was telling the others that he was only dating her so he could get close to some of the contacts she had in the entertainment business.

He joked that being with her was like hanging out with his kid sister. She wasn't much bigger, either! The others made snide remarks, wanting to know if he had bedded the 'baby'. He had jokingly told them he tried, but he didn't fit in the crib she slept in. She was about to give him a piece of her mind again when she was pulled away into the misty swirling colors again. She spun around floating upward until she reached another time in her life.

Now, she was at the cabin in the mountains she had rented for her, Jo, and River. She and Jo were talking excitedly about what they were going to do once River joined them. It had been almost a year since they were able to get together with River Knight, their best friend and adopted sister.

The three of them had grown up together traveling with the circus. They had been inseparable and they missed her so much since they had stopped traveling. Life on the road had lost some of its glamor for Jo and Star after their parents retired. They still performed in a circus doing their death-defying aerial stunts, but they did it without moving around. When their parents retired to Florida, Jo and Star had stayed with the circus family they had grown up with for a couple years before joining Circus of the Stars in Orlando, Florida. Here they expanded their performances to include aerial stunts mixed with incredible special effects.

Star moved restlessly as the mists in her dream turned darker. Memories now invaded her dreams. There had been a sound on the front porch of the cabin they were renting. Star thought it was River.

A cry ripped from her throat as the dark, alien figure appeared in front of her. She struggled weakly against the hands holding her, fighting to break free, but she couldn't get her body to do what she wanted it to do. A soothing voice filtered through before it faded as the cloak of dark mist spun its web around her until she was swept away on its dark waves.

* * *

Jazin stared up at Shavic who was injecting Star with a sedative. "What is happening? Is she in pain? Why can't you help her?" He asked with a worried frown as he ran a soothing hand along the side of her face.

He glanced down, watching as her face relaxed as she slipped further down into a more restful sleep. It had been touch and go for the first few hours. One of the healers had even come for him to be near her side when they thought she wouldn't make it at one point. He had clung to her hand, demanding that she obey him for once. He would not tolerate her not fighting.

He refused to believe that he could lose her. She meant too much to him.

Shavic, his brother's healer from aboard his warship, came in a short time later ordering him back out until he had time to evaluate Star. His older brother, Torak, had called him. He trusted Shavic more than any other except the healer who had worked on River when she was injured. It was only because that healer was unavailable that he relied on Shavic. Two hours passed before Shavic tiredly walked back into the waiting room where Jazin, Ajaska, Manota, Jo, Madas, and her mate, Gril, were waiting. Torak, with River by his side, was being seen by another healer. He had also been injured during the attack that night.

Jazin almost broke down in front of everyone when Shavic told him Star would make it. She would need plenty of rest and time to rebuild her strength, but she would be fine. Manota had taken Jo back to their house, ignoring her protests that she wanted to stay with her sister. She only relented when she saw the barely controlled emotion on Jazin's face. He vaguely remembered his father, Madas and Gril giving him a comforting squeeze on his arm before they left him to follow Shavic back to Star's bedside.

That had been almost an hour ago. Shavic was still monitoring Star. When she began moving restlessly in the bed and moaning, he decided it would be best if she remained sedated for a while longer to give her additional time to heal. Shavic said there had been some progress on upgrading the equipment to handle the human anatomy, but they were still learning. The biggest breakthrough had been the synthetic blood source they were able to develop that was compatible with the humans.

"Your mate has lost a lot of blood. It will take time to replenish it. I do not want to give her too much yet. I want to make sure she does not have a reaction," Shavic said. "She is not in pain. The pain inhibitors on her temple prevent that. She is merely dreaming."

"You are sure she will make it?" Jazin asked quietly, gazing down at Star's pale face.

Shavic laid the injector down on the tray and looked at Jazin before turning his gaze to Star. "She will make it. She is strong and she is a fighter. She will recover," he repeated confidently. "She will sleep for several more hours. Why don't you get cleaned up and get some rest?"

Jazin stared defiantly at Shavic. "I won't leave her."

Shavic chuckled. "Use the cleansing unit here. You can rest next to her," he said with a nod to the bed. "It opens further."

Jazin nodded. "You will stay with her until I return?" He asked hesitantly, unwilling to leave her alone for even a minute.

"Go," Shavic said gently. "I will stay with her. Your captain of the guard brought you a change of clothes."

Jazin rose reluctantly, letting his fingers linger on Star's cheek. "She is so headstrong," he murmured.

"All three of the human females are. I should have known they were up to something."

"What do you think their world is like?" Shavic asked in wonder, staring at Star's pale, peaceful face as she rested. "Do you think all the women there are warriors like them?"

Jazin looked at Shavic, a small smile pulled at the corner of his mouth. Now that he knew Star would make it, he felt calmer by a small measure. He thought of the video he saw of Star when she was younger. Her friend, River, had a set of video disks and his brother, Torak, had asked him to copy them to a format that devices on their world could read. Neither he nor his brothers expected to discover what they had. The women were not warriors. They were performers who did incredible feats.

No, they were not warriors in the true sense but they were warriors when it came to protecting those they loved and cared about, Jazin thought as he watched Star's lips part in a deep sigh. *They fought with an ingenuity and skill that belied their delicate forms.*

"I don't know," Jazin replied, momentarily frozen in the fact that he truly did not know much about his mate or her world.

Shavic shrugged. "It does not matter. They are all incredible. Go get cleaned up, Lord Jazin. I will watch over your mate until you return," he said with a hint of compassion.

Shavic recognized that Jazin needed time to deal with what had happened. He could not blame him. If he had a mate as beautiful, fierce, and loyal as Jazin did, he would have reacted the same if anything happened to her.

Shavic sank down wearily into the chair next to the bed and studied the delicate face of the human female. Since his first encounter with them, he had been fascinated by their differences to the known species he had treated. There were over twenty star systems in the Alliance. Each star system had their own unique species, some like the Kassis and some vastly different like the Tearnats.

The human females were the first that were closely related in features to their own. He gently picked up the delicate hand laying on the edge of the bed and turned it over to study her palm. Her fingers twitched as his light touch. A wave of envy flooded him. To feel hands like these on his body, running their tips....

"I will stay with her now," Jazin's hard voice said from behind Shavic.

* * *

Jazin kept a tight rein on his emotions. He had taken a brief shower and changed into clean clothing as fast as he could, not wanting to be away from his mate's side any longer than necessary. A deep fear gnawed at him that he had only dreamed that Star would be alright.

When he had returned, a dark jealousy swept through him at seeing Shavic tenderly holding Star's hand. He had watched Shavic's face intensely for a moment while the healer caressed it. Emotions of confusion, envy, and desire flowed across the man's face unhindered by the normally calm mask he wore.

Shavic gently laid Star's hand back down before he stood; the mask of impassive calm once again on his face. "My lord," he responded quietly before bowing and leaving the room.

Jazin watched through narrow eyes as Shavic left before turning back to his mate. He moved over to the bed and swiped his hand over the panel above it. The bed shifted, expanding until it was large enough to accommodate his larger frame.

He pulled back the covers and lowered himself onto the bed, making sure he didn't jar it any more than necessary. He carefully lifted Star's body so he could pull her against his long length. He marveled at their difference in size and how she fit perfectly against him. He lowered his head until his chin rested against the sweet smelling strands of her hair. Taking a deep breath, he drew in the scent of wild flowers and sunlight.

He would never get enough of her. From the first moment he saw her on the Tearnat's warship, he knew he was lost. His eyes drifted shut as relief, mixed with exhaustion from fear and battle, washed through him. His body relaxed as Star turned into his warmth, seeking the safe haven of his arms even in her unconscious state. It had been her beautiful eyes that had first caught his attention. They spoke of love and laughter. Of hope, wonder, and curiosity. Of power and strength. Of peace and forever.

Sleep called to Jazin as he continued breathing in the calming scent of his mate. His mind drifted to the first time he saw her coming out of the darkened corridor. A tiny warrior who would touch not only his heart, but his entire world.

Colors and images swirled and solidified as his dream formed. It was as if he were an apparition reliving a moment in time. They had been on a diplomatic mission with the *Krail*, the current Chancellor for the Alliance. Their shuttle was on its way to intercept Torak's warship when a rebel group of Tearnats fired upon them, taking out their engines.

Trolis, the leader of the rebel group and second son of Madas and Gril Tal Mod, had killed the chancellor and taken Jazin, Torak and the other eight warriors' prisoner. Trolis planned to kill them all, starting with Jazin. He wanted to set an example for the other members of the Alliance by eliminating two of the most powerful royals of Kassis.

Jazin remembered waking up, chained between two bars used for interrogation. Progit, a Tearnat warrior Torak had disfigured during the war, came in. Jazin buried his nose deeper into the tantalizing scent of his mate's hair. He remembered the feel of the sharp blade as it caressed his cheek, cutting a line down it. Progit was bragging about how he was going to kill him. He was going to cut him apart, one limb at a time. Jazin had been sure it was his time to die. He had braced himself for the first blow, determined to die a warrior's death and not give the Tearnat the pleasure of hearing him scream in agony as he was dismembered. Instead, it was Progit who collapsed at his feet…. a knife between his eyes.

Jazin moved restlessly in his sleep, drawing the body pressed against him closer. *Star…* He had learned her name from the dark haired female that captured his older brother's attention. River Knight had killed the three Tearnats in the room with several well-thrown blades.

She had approached him first to see how badly he was wounded. While she had captured his attention due to her unexpected and unusual appearance, he didn't feel anything more than curiosity. Nothing had prepared him for his first glance at the one she called Star, though.

He remembered the feeling well. It was as if someone had punched him in the stomach. Even now, he still had the same reaction as the first time he saw her.

His lips curved as he remembered her petite figure coming to stand in front of him. She had been hesitant to touch him and had glared at him in warning to not try anything. He had been so mesmerized by her pale beauty that all he could think was she was his!

She had cleaned his wound, trying hard not to touch his skin. He, on the other hand, had craved her touch from the first moment he looked into her light blue eyes. Even then she had glowered at him defiantly. She had a stubborn tilt to her small, delicate chin and a look in her eyes that dared him to mess with her even as she gently cleaned the blood away from his wound. He knew it wasn't bad. It stung, but he had received worse injuries during the war. Progit had merely been teasing him with what was to come.

He had fought to reach for her, but couldn't with his arms still shackled to the bars holding him. She had whispered quietly to him. Four simple words, but he would never forget them.

"You are safe now," her husky voice whispered, burning into his soul as if it was lit from within.

She had disappeared shortly after that. The females had done the unthinkable. They had set Jazin, Torak and the other warriors free and disabled the huge warship, giving his brother, Manota, a chance to overtake it.

Star had worked her way through the warship disabling the exits to the living quarter levels, trapping the Tearnats so they couldn't fight. His heart had clenched in fear when the time passed for the females to appear in the docking bay. He had been surprised to find Manota had not traveled alone.

Gril Tal Mod, Trolis' father and leader of the Tearnats, had come with his own warriors. He was furious, but not surprised, that his second son would disobey a direct order. Trolis had tried to kill him at one point towards the end of the war when Gril wanted peace for his species.

Trolis had escaped and built a small but impressive army of mercenaries, disgruntled warriors unhappy with the peace, and loyal supporters. He had died on the warship when he attacked Torak and Gril. Another victim of the sharp blades his new sister loved to carry.

One dream after another flowed in an endless spiral through time; Star on board his brother's Starship, her face when she appeared in the docking bay before the councilman who would later betray them, the moment when she had felt deceived by him for having his House filled with women. One memory after another floated through his mind. Even her outraged face when he threw her over his shoulder and claimed her officially as his before his people.

She had only begun to warm to him before tonight. She was afraid of something. She refused to tell him, but he could feel the hesitation whenever he held her and murmured words of need. Scene after scene filled the next several hours as he held her tightly in his arms before he drifted into the realm between the worlds of dreams and wakefulness.

Jazin jerked awake when he felt a presence entering the room. His hand moved instinctively to the laser sword next to him under the covers. His eyes moved to his Captain of the Guard as Armet came in. He frowned, shaking his head. Armet bowed and motioned that he would remain outside. Jazin glanced down at the warm figure in his arms and nodded.

He waited until Armet left before he slowly disentangled himself from the body now lying more on top of him than beside. He brushed a soft kiss over Star's forehead before he carefully rose out of the bed and tucked the covers securely around her. He glanced at her once more before he turned to leave the room. Her face was flushed a dusty rose and a slight smile curved her lips. He wondered what she was dreaming of and could only hope it had something to do with him.

Chapter 3

"Armet," Jazin said as he quietly closed the door behind him.

"My lord. Please forgive my intrusion," Armet bowed respectfully. "Your brothers and father wish for you to meet with them. They expressed their regret but new information has come to their attention that they feel you should know about."

Jazin's mouth tightened. He glanced at the door. He had only been asleep for a few hours, but it had been enough to refresh him. Still, he was hesitant to leave his mate. His eyes moved to the door as it opened. Jo, Star's sister, and River walked through the entrance talking quietly. They both paused, looking anxiously at him.

"Star?" Jo asked in a husky voice.

"She is sleeping peacefully and looks much better," Jazin replied. "I would thank you to let her rest as long as possible. Shavic said it is the best thing for her at this time."

Jo rolled her eyes. "I figured that. I was just worried she...." Jo drew in a deep breath and smiled tearfully at River who wound her arm around her waist in support. "I was just worried."

Jazin relaxed slightly as he noted the pinched look around Jo's mouth. He knew she loved her little sister and was very protective. That was evident the few times he had seen them together. In fact, he saw how all three were very supportive and protective of each other. His thoughts flitted to his own father and brothers and he had a deeper appreciation for his own relationship with them. He had never thought of it much before now. Thinking of his father and brothers reminded him that they were waiting for him.

"I trust you ladies to stay and watch over my mate until I can return," Jazin said. "I am needed in a meeting. Armet will stay outside the rooms if you should need anything."

Armet looked startled for a moment before he nodded. He had grown attached to the little female who had taken over the Third House of Kassis, also known as the West House. He had to admit it was much easier to maintain since she had come.

He would have never complained, but he and several of the warriors under his command had their hands full at times dealing with the females who used to live in the West House. Those remaining now were either mated, children, or older couples. The little female often visited each of the families to see how they were doing and if they needed anything. He was also fascinated by some of the things that she could do. He had never seen anyone move the way she did in the training room and some of the things she created were not only innovative but useful.

"I will return as soon as possible," Jazin was saying.

He gave a sharp look to Armet. Armet nodded to show he was aware of the unspoken command; protect all three females with his life. Armet spoke quietly into his comlink and moved to stand by the door as Jazin cast one last, longing look at the door leading to the room where his mate slept.

"Protect them," Jazin muttered under his breath as he walked out the door.

"With my life, my lord," Armet said with a glitter of pride and respect in his eyes. "With my life."

* * *

Star woke up in stages. The first stage, she became aware that there was light filtering into the room. The second stage, she became aware of the soft sound of voices murmuring beside her. The last stage and the most important one was she became aware that she didn't hurt... anywhere. She flexed her toes back and forth before moving her legs. When she still didn't feel any pain, she moved her fingers before turning her head toward the voices and opening her eyes.

Twin sets of eyes, one an unusual dark blue and the other a set of light blue like her own, stared at her with worry and love gleaming from them. Star slowly smiled before she whispered in a husky voice.

"Hi," she murmured.

River grinned back. Jo opened her mouth, closed it, and promptly burst into tears. Star's eyes widened as she watched her older sister's shoulders shake as she cried. River was pressing a small towel into Jo's hands and hugging her.

"Is she hurt?" Star asked, her voice raspy from being dry.

She struggled to sit up so she could comfort her big sister and was surprised that it wasn't that easy to do. She finally made it into an upright position, balancing herself on her arms until her head stopped spinning.

"Wow!" Star muttered, raising a trembling hand to her head. "Head rush."

"You dope! You shouldn't be sitting up yet," Jo bit out between hiccuping sobs. "You were dead almost twenty-four hours ago. You shouldn't even be.... be.... be able to sit up."

"Water?" Star asked with a grimace, rubbing her throat.

River reached over and picked up a small cup of water that was on the table next to the bed. She held the cup while Star took several small sips from it before she set it back down on the table. Jo's sobs slowly became quieter until she was just drawing in deep, calming breaths. Jo wiped at her reddened cheeks with the soft cloth that was clutched in her fist in aggravation.

When she felt like she finally had a small semblance of control back, she glared at her little sister. "Don't you ever scare me like that again!" Jo snapped out, wiping at her still damp cheeks.

Star chuckled as she weakly collapsed back against the pillows. "It's not like I planned to get hurt," she said. "Jazin?" She asked fearfully.

"He's safe," River assured her with a smile.

"What happened?" Star asked, looking back and forth between River and Jo. "Was anyone else hurt?"

River bit her lip and looked at Jo, who nodded. "Yes," River began quietly. "Eighteen people were killed in the banquet room. Most were women on the stage and several of the men who were sitting close to it. Thirty men who attacked us were killed. Javonna was working with them. She is dead, as well," she said quietly.

"What about the councilman? Tai Tek?" Star asked, nervously playing with the covers.

Jo shook her head. "He escaped," she said, her lips pressed into a tight line of frustration. "If I ever get my hands on that bastard, I'm going to barbeque his ass over an open flame."

Star laughed at Jo's fierce scowl. "Was anyone else hurt? Ajaska? Manota? Torak?" She asked biting her lower lip in concern.

River reached over and gripped one of Star's hands. "Torak was hurt when he fought one of the Tearnat's guarding Tai Tek but not seriously. None of the others were hurt," she assured.

"Jazin was frantic when he saw you….," Jo's voice choked up again.

"We came very close to losing you, Star," River continued. "You scared all of us, especially Jazin. He really does love you."

Star sniffed and looked away. "He's never said he does. He just says I'm his and I should do what he tells me to do," she grumbled under her breath. "Fat chance that is ever going to happen."

River giggled. "I can always lend you my knives if you need them. Once I pinned Torak to the door with them, he's been very careful about his 'I'm the man' speech ever since," she giggled.

Star's lips turned up in a smile. She looked at her surrogate sister with a twinkle in her eye. The thought of pinning Jazin to the door brought up some interesting ideas. She just might have to take River up on her offer if he became too overbearing again.

"So how long have I been out and what has happened since everything went fuzzy on me?" Star asked tiredly. "And why in the hell do I feel like I've been hit by a truck?"

"It wasn't a truck, but a laser blast to the back," Jo snapped out. "It's a miracle you are even moving right now. If Madas hadn't gotten you to medical as fast as she did, you wouldn't be here," she gritted out as tears filled her eyes again. "Damn it! Now I'm crying again."

* * *

Three weeks later, Star was seriously thinking about borrowing River's knives. Jazin had ordered all the guards to make sure she was protected at all times when he couldn't be with her. He was busy working on some 'top secret' defense system most of the day.

From the little bit she had been able to gather, which wasn't much, Tai Tek was preparing for another attack. This time, he had approached another alien star system outside the Alliance's jurisdiction. The species wasn't well known as they kept primarily to themselves. Rumors, or Intel that was coming in, stated Tai Tek had promised unlimited access to the planet's energy crystal mines in exchange for help in defeating the Houses of Kassis.

Jazin had been working with Manota on a defense system to protect not only their planet but their warships. While Manota's shield worked at protecting the four royal houses, Jazin's would protect their fleet of warships during battle. In the meantime, while he was busy, he had ordered Star to rest as much as possible.

River and Jo came over daily to visit but she was not allowed to even set foot out of the West House. Hell, even the healer that saved River came to her. When she had asked why Shavic wasn't still caring for her, Jazin's eyes had turned a darker black and he had said that Shavic had been reassigned back to the warship.

In the meantime, she had snuck out of the house at least a dozen times and each time, either Armet or Jazin caught her. And each and every exit she used was then either barred or a guard placed in front of it. She was really beginning to get desperate.

It was time to break out the knives, she thought with glee as the picture of Jazin stuck to the door floated through her mind.

A knock on the door roused Star from her dark, gleeful thoughts. She let out a deep sigh and hoped it was her sister and River. She knew River had to be careful right now since she was pregnant but that didn't mean she couldn't help Star escape the confines of the house. She was going batty being locked up!

The knock sounded again as Star approached. "I'm coming. I'm coming. Keep your pantyhose on," Star called out in frustration.

She opened the door and stood back in shock when she saw Madas Tal Mod standing outside the door. The huge Tearnat's lips pulled back to reveal a set of even, but very sharp, teeth. Star's eyebrow rose. It was probably the closest thing to a smile a Tearnat could make, she guessed.

"Hi Madas," Star said in surprise. She glanced around to see if there was anyone else with her. "Would you like to come in?"

"That is usually what happens when someone requests entrance into a room," Madas teased.

Star chuckled. She liked the big female Tearnat. Not just because she saved her life, but because she did have a wicked sense of humor.

"I guess you are right," Star laughed as she opened the door further. She waited patiently as Madas entered, sniffing the air as she came through. "What brings you here? Jo and River wouldn't have happened to send you here to rescue me, would they?" She asked hopefully.

Madas turned in an elegant circle to look darkly at Star. "You need help?" She growled out menacingly. "The Kassis lord is mistreating you?"

Star released a deep sigh and shook her head. She motioned with one hand for Madas to have a seat on the long, dark burgundy couch in the center of their living area. Star sat down on a matching chair across from her. There was a small, delicately carved crystal table between them. A refreshment tray containing hot tea, dozens of small pastries and breads, and a mixture of fresh fruit had been brought in earlier.

"Not unless being kept on a pedestal is considered mistreatment," Star reluctantly responded. She reached over and poured Madas and herself some tea. "Would you like some pastries, bread, or fruit? They always bring me way too much. Plus, it isn't much fun eating alone all the time."

Madas reached over and gingerly took the small cup of hot liquid from Star. She then proceeded to load a plate full of each of the items. She always did like the food and drink on this planet. It was one of the few that reminded her of her home.

Madas grinned when she saw Star's eyes widened at the size of the helping on her plate. "I am much larger than you, little warrior, and never turn down the delicious food available here. It reminds me of my home. My clan lives at the edge of the great mountains. We grow much of our own food there. Fruit hangs heavy from the trees that surround our village and the grasses along the snow ridges are used to make breads. We are careful of the amount of meat we eat. Gril's clan comes from closer to the desert where there is not an abundance of such things. His clan survives primarily on the flesh of the animals that live in the region," Madas explained.

Star looked at the huge dark green, brown, and black creature closely. She could see the beauty in the way her skin formed into soft scales. Her head was delicately curved with a series of ridges along the top that flowed down like waves of hair. Her skin was very soft and dry, not hard and wet like she had expected. She wore a long-sleeved light tan shirt with a darker brown vest over it and soft, dark brown pants tucked into mid-calf length, soft brown boots. Around each wrist was a band of what looked like gold. Her claw-like fingers were slender and the nails, while very long, were carefully manicured. Her long tail wound down along her side and the tip curled around one ankle like a cape.

"You are very beautiful," Star murmured out loud before she blushed in embarrassment.

Madas chuckled as she leaned back. "Thank you, little warrior. It is not often that other species look beyond what they want to see. Most think of the Tearnats as a savage species with little culture or capacity for caring," Madas said, her eyes sad for a moment. "I am just as guilty. When I first saw Gril....," her husky, warm voice faded as a small rose color filled her face.

"Oh no you don't," Star said in fascination. "You are so not going to start and not finish! How did you two meet?"

Madas blushed again and looked down at the plate in her lap. "He was on a training mission. The single fighter ship he was in developed engine problems and he was forced to land. He had never been to the mountainous regions of our home world before. My clan was very isolated at the time. My mother led our clan after my father died. In our clan, the females were taught to fight as well as the males.

My mother believed it was important that all members of the clan be ready to defend it if necessary. There are many animals that live in the mountains that would not hesitate to attack. We were excellent hunters and trackers. I learned how to use the plants to heal from my grandmother." Madas paused to take a small bite out of the fresh fruit on her plate. Her eyes closed briefly as the sweet juice flowed down her throat. When her eyes opened, they glittered with humor. "I saw Gril's fighter landing in a meadow half a mountain away from our village. I rushed to see what it was as I had never seen one before. When he stepped out of it and turned, I thought I had never seen an uglier male in my life!"

"You thought Gril was ugly?" Star asked amazed.

Madas chuckled. "You have to understand, I had never seen a male like him before. He was all muscle and he was bigger and paler than the males of our clan. He gets his coloring from the desert."

Star nodded. She had wondered why Gril was so much lighter than Madas. He also had just one ridge on his head and his teeth were longer and sharper. His coloring was more like the color of the desert camouflage outfits that the military wore back home.

"So, what happened?" Star asked impatiently. "What did he do when he saw you?"

"He didn't.... at first," Madas responded with a glint in her eyes. "Remember, he was in my territory. I knew how to hunt, track, and remain hidden. I was the best warrior in our clan and the daughter of the leader. But, I underestimated his ability to sense he was not alone. He is very good at trusting his instincts and he had experienced war where I had not. For two days, we played with each other. He would disappear, trying to circle around me while I would stay one step ahead of him. I grew to respect his skills as he came closer and closer to me." Her voice grew warm as her memories flooded her. "On the third day, he caught me. He had set a trap and I walked into it."

Star was staring at Madas totally mesmerized by the story. Her hand reached up to her throat. What must it have been like to have the huge Tearnat stalking her day after day? Then, to be caught in a trap, unable to get out. Star could feel her own pulse increase at the thought.

"What did you do?" Star breathed out.

Madas grinned. "I cursed him, fought him, and fell in love with him," she said quietly.

"Yes, but....," Star grounded her teeth together. "What did he do?"

Madas' cheeks burned with color as she lowered her head. "He claimed me. Over and over until I couldn't think straight. Then, he demanded I take him back to my clan so he could tell them I belonged to him," she hissed out softly.

"How did your mom feel about him?" Star asked curiously, wondering how her own parents would react to Jazin's claim on her.

"She insisted he prove that he was strong enough to claim me," Madas replied, looking out the window as she remembered how frightened she had been. "In my clan, a warrior has to prove he is strong enough to protect his mate. If he is not, both die. I was taken during the night to the Death Springs. Gril had three days to find and rescue me."

"What do you mean, you would both die? What happens at the Death Springs?" Star asked quietly, sensing this was not a good thing.

Madas looked intently at Star before she lowered her eyes. "There is a place in the mountains where the heat of the planet is closer to the surface. There are springs in this area where the water boils and nothing can live. My clan uses these springs as a test. Cages are suspended above the largest boiling spring and the male or female who is being claimed is placed in it. For three days and three nights, they are left there alone. If the warrior claiming them does not complete the journey to the Death Springs before the light of the fourth day, the cage is lowered into the boiling water," Madas explained quietly. "The path to the springs is deadly. Many warriors have lost their lives trying to make it. Even then, some have made the journey, but did not arrive in time to save their mate. If they survive, but their mate does not, they are given to the boiling waters for failing to be a good protector."

"But Gril made it," Star insisted. "He saved you, otherwise you wouldn't be here now."

Madas smiled. "Yes, he made it. My clan was not happy that I was claimed by a warrior from outside the clan. They...." Madas shook her head sadly. "Tell me why you are unhappy, little warrior. Perhaps I can help you."

Star realized there was more to the story of Madas and Gril but she also realized that she would not get any more today. They spent the next several hours talking about Star's frustration at getting Jazin to realize that she might be small but she was strong. Madas laughed as she told Star about the night she was injured. She told her how she had warned Jazin that there were some forces in the universe he couldn't control. One of them was his mate.

Madas promised that if Star really wanted to get out for a while, all she had to do was call. Madas would be more than happy to sneak her out. After all, she was forever doing it to Gril! Star gave her big, alien friend a fierce hug before she left. This world really wasn't so different from the one she had known in the circus. Friends came in all different sizes, shapes, and forms there as well.

Chapter 4

"Jazin, I have to return to Earth and tell my parents Jo and I are alright. I was thinking maybe...," Star said later that night. She stared into the mirror and shook her head. "No, I'm not going to tell him I'm thinking maybe," she sighed in frustration. "Since when did you ever ask to do something, girl? You are not growing weak and needy! Walter would turn me over his knee and spank my ass if I became a wimp," she growled out to her reflection.

"No one is going to turn you over and spank you, but me," a dark growl came from behind her.

Star squeaked in surprise. She had been so busy trying to figure out the best way to approach Jazin about taking her back to Earth that she didn't hear him come in. It was late, well after midnight. It was always late when he came in lately. Since she had been injured, he insisted on her sharing his bed. She refused for all the fat lot of good it did her. She went to bed in her bed and either woke up in his or he was in hers.

She was just so afraid he was going to turn out to be like Justin, her first real boyfriend. She felt like she had been in a cocoon her entire life until she and Jo got their condo in Orlando. It was kind-of difficult to go on a date or get serious about anyone when you were in a different city every other night. Not to mention, she had more surrogate aunts, uncles, and grandparents than any kid needed as a chaperone. In Orlando, she and Jo had lived with their parents for the first year after they gave up the circus. They wanted to make sure it was something they really wanted to do. She had been so consumed with learning the new routines and adapting to life outside of the small world of the circus that she didn't even think about dating.

The past year was the first time she felt comfortable with the idea of going out. She had only gone out on a couple of dates before she met Justin. He had joined the performing troupe three months before they were kidnapped. Star had immediately been smitten with his handsome, blonde looks.

It took two more months before he asked her out. She should have known something was up when he didn't even give her a second glance until a Nighttime Entertainment crew came to film her and Jo performing. The producer of NTE was doing a documentary on the Strauss Family Flyers to promote a film that Star and Jo had been in. After that, Justin was all over her. She was glad she had been nervous about taking their relationship to the next level so soon after he asked her out.

She wanted what her parents had, a loving, long term relationship. She was having second thoughts about whether she should just go ahead and let Justin make love to her before he made any commitment to her. After all, the girls in the performing troupe were always talking about the guys they had 'done' the night before.

She was reluctant because that wasn't the way she had been raised. Thank goodness she had overheard the conversation between Justin and several of the other cast members before she made that mistake! She had been on the catwalk above them, checking the rigging before that night's performance. The sound of their voices had drifted upwards and she heard every cruel word the people she thought were her friends said.

She had broken down and told Jo what happened. That next night, her and Jo resigned after their performance. They would meet up with River and let her know they were rejoining the circus. It was where they both fit in.

Star took a deep breath and turned to face Jazin. She refused to back down. He needed to accept her for herself or their relationship could never go any further. Her eyes swept over his black hair that was clipped back at the nape.

He towered over her petite five feet two inches, but she had never been intimidated by anyone taller than her. Walter had shown her that size didn't matter if you wanted something. She bit her bottom lip as she stared into his dark, almost black eyes.

She had never seen eyes that dark before and felt like she could drown in them. His face was defined by sharp but handsome lines. She would have thought his darker colors came from working outside in the sun if not for the fact she had seen the dark coloring disappearing below the waist of his low-hung black pants in the mornings.

His eyes were the color of midnight on a moonless night, a small sliver of silver light shimmered in the center. His strong nose and full lips called to her and made her frustrated with her own insecurities. She wanted to give in to him. She had from the first moment she gazed into his eyes on the Tearnat warship. It was only the uncertainty of what was to become of her and her sister that held her back. She had no doubt at all that River was never going to return to Earth. The key difference between River and her and Jo was that River had no other family to return to.

Star closed her eyes briefly at the wave of pain that swept through her at the thought of how heartbroken her parents would be/were. The idea of losing one daughter would be horrendous but to think that both of their daughters were missing and presumed dead was beyond the realm of sanity.

"What is it?" Jazin asked anxiously. "Are you in pain? Should I call for the healer?"

Tears filled Star's eyes and she cursed the fact that she had always been a cry baby when she was upset. "No, I'm not in pain. At least not a physical pain," she whispered. "Jazin, I miss my parents. I can't help but think about what they must be going through. The idea of losing one daughter is tragic, but to lose both of your children has to be unbearable for them. I can't imagine what they must be going through. They must know by now that something happened to us. We've never gone this long without calling them."

Jazin looked down into the pain filled eyes of his mate. His hand rose gently to touch her cheek. "Your sister has said as much to Manota," he sighed heavily.

"She will not commit to him until she can assure your parents that you are both safe."

Star jerked in surprise. Jo never mentioned a word to her about her relationship with Manota or the fact that she had been pressuring him to contact their parents in some way. She was getting really tired of people keeping things from her. Just because she was small and had been hurt that didn't mean she should be kept in the dark.

"What are you and your brother going to do?" Star asked with a stubborn tilt to her chin. "I won't let them spend the rest of their lives grieving for us. You can't expect either Jo or I to do that. If your father thought…." Her sharp words faded as Jazin drew her closer to him with a groan of need.

He loved it when she had that fire in her eyes. He couldn't resist her any longer. The last of his tightly held control dissolved as he felt her body melt into his. He had given her time on the warship to adjust to what had happened to her and to come to terms with the loss of everything she knew but her sister and friend.

Once on Kassis, she had fought him harder than any warrior he had ever encountered before when he had taken her to his House. Her world did not accept the same levels of class recognition as his did. She had stormed out of his House crying when he had been greeted by the females who lived there. It was considered a level of strength, power and wealth for a male to have many women in his home. Star did not appreciate his status at all. In fact, the hurt and rage in her eyes had burned through him, leaving him feeling anything but proud.

When an assassin's charge almost took the life of his brother's mate, he had learned that human females did not share – ever. Star's refusal to return to his House had him rethinking things. She had finally moved into his House just a few weeks ago. Even then, she had only begun to warm up to him the last few days before the dinner and subsequent attack.

Jazin pulled away slightly to gaze down into the passion-filled eyes of his mate. "Manota is going to take Jo back for your parents. Kev Mul Kar, Torak's Captain of the Guard, will go with them. He has returned from his mission. He is familiar with the Tearnat's navigational charts. We have the location of your planet from Trolis' warship. Our technology is more advanced than the Tearnat and the trip should take about half the time it took before to return once they have secured your parents," Jazin explained huskily.

Star looked up at Jazin in shock before a huge grin lit her face with happiness. She threw her arms around Jazin's waist and hugged him tightly. Her parents were going to be totally shocked, but they would be happy as long as they knew she and Jo were.

Several things dawned on her as she held Jazin tightly against her. First, he and Manota wouldn't bother doing this if they didn't really care for her and Jo. Second, he was very much aroused if the bulge pressing against her stomach was any indication of his feelings for her. And third, she wanted him with a fierce desire that was eating away at her. She had from the first moment she heard his husky voice telling his brother goodbye.

She pulled back, a rosy hue coloring her cheeks as she stared at his chest. "You.... Ah.... Your....," She drew in a deep breath and shyly looked up at him. "You're aroused."

Jazin's eyes lit with laughter as he loosely held her in front of him. "I have been aroused since the first moment I saw you on board Trolis' warship," he admitted huskily.

"Well," Star said, looking nervously up at him. "I guess we should do something about that, shouldn't we?"

It took a moment for Jazin to realize what Star was saying. He had gotten so used to her saying 'no' that his brain seemed to short-circuit for a second or two. He closed his eyes as a shaft of painful need flooded him. His nose twitched as the tantalizing scent of her arousal penetrated his consciousness.

Gods, he thought as he fought to get control of his suddenly hypersensitive body. *I want her so badly that I'm afraid.*

"Jazin?" The soft question in her voice drew his eyes to hers again.

"I, Jazin Ja Kel Coradon of the Third House of Kassis, claim you, Star, for my house and as my mate. I claim you as my woman. No other may claim you. I will kill any other who try. I give you my protection as is my right as leader of my house. I claim you as is my right by the House of Kassis," Jazin said quietly as he brushed Star's beautiful blond hair back from her face with trembling fingers. "I'm never going to let you go, Star."

Star's eyes filled with tears. She bit her lower lip and took a step closer to his warm body. "Do you promise, Jazin? Forever?"

"Oh yes," he breathed out knowing she could never understand just how much she meant to him. "You are my heart, Star. You are the woman I have given it to and the only one who will ever have it," Jazin vowed solemnly.

Star reached up and touched his cheek with the tips of her fingers. "I claim you, Jazin. As my partner, as my friend, as my husband. Love me," she whispered.

"You are sure?" He asked, the muscle in his jaw clenched tightly as he held onto his control by a thread. "I am not sure I could stop once...." His voice faded as she gently laid her fingers against his lips.

"I won't change my mind," she promised.

To prove her point, she took a step back and reached for the clasp holding the robe covering her. She released the crystal catch and the robe parted, revealing the sheer gown she wore underneath it. She shrugged her shoulders, letting the silky material fall to pool around her slender ankles.

Jazin's breath caught in his throat as he felt the fire in his blood heat to boiling. He stepped forward, sweeping her up into his arms. Striding down the corridor to his rooms, he pushed the door open with his shoulder not stopping until he could lower her petite frame down onto the silky covers. He followed, pressing his lips frantically to hers in a deep kiss that promised an explosion of passion and need that would take both of their breaths away.

Jazin's mind was splintering as he pressed down on Star's petite form. He knew he should go slow but his body could only think of claiming her as his for all time. Feelings washed through him as her taste swept through him like the waves crashing to shore on a newly formed beach. His fingers tangled frantically in her hair before moving down her to skim her face. His fingers continued their descent until he reached the strap of the sheer gown she was wearing. With a low groan, he snapped the strap with a quick tug. His seeking fingers trembled as they touched her heated flesh. He swallowed her moan as he pushed the offending material further down. He broke the kiss with a shuddering gasp and sat up, pinning her body between his muscular thighs.

"You are so beautiful," he breathed out as he gripped the torn top of her gown and pulled it down to reveal her small, perky breasts to his feasting eyes.

"Jazin," Star whispered huskily, staring up into his eyes. "Love me."

Jazin smiled as he ran his roughened palms down over the sensitive swell of her breasts before he rolled her tender nipples between his fingers. His smile grew as she arched upward with a startled gasp. He pinched her nipples just hard enough to draw a heated groan from her.

"These are mine," he whispered softly. "Tell me. Tell me they are mine. Tell me they only belong to me."

Star continued looking up into the blazing eyes staring down at her with such passion a lump formed in her throat. She opened her mouth to answer him, but a soft moan escaped her parted lips instead when he pinched the swollen tips harder. She swallowed and nodded instead as she bowed under him, her hands reaching up to grasp his thighs.

"Say it," he hissed as he rolled them again and ground his swollen cock against her belly. "Tell me that they are mine."

"They…." She swallowed again before continuing. "They are yours. Only yours. Forever."

"Put your hands above your head," he said, massaging the small globes in his palms.

Star hesitated for a second before she raised her arms above her head. The movement forced her breasts higher. Jazin leaned forward, taking first one nipple, then the other into his mouth and sucking until both were hard and achy.

"Please," Star moaned huskily, closing her eyes as the tugging on her nipples pulled at something deep inside her she had never felt before. Her legs moved restlessly as her pussy clenched. "Please."

Jazin pulled his lips reluctantly from the taut nipple he was tormenting. "Do you trust me?" He whispered.

Star's eyes flew open at the intense question. He was asking her for total surrender. He was asking her to give herself to him totally, without restraint, without question, wholly. For a moment fear rose to choke her. What if he just used her and tossed her aside? What if she was making a mistake? Could she trust him completely? Could she give him everything, including her heart? She stared up into his dark eyes, searching and knew without a doubt what the answer was....

"Yes," she said never breaking her gaze from his. "Yes, I trust you."

Jazin released the breath he had been holding and smoothed the tangle of blond hair back from her face with a trembling hand. He swore silently that he would never give her an opportunity to regret her decision.

He reached up behind the headboard of his bed and grasped the soft, restraints he had attached to it several days before. He had known he was reaching the end of his endurance and had installed the restraints with the idea of having to convince Star to lose her control. Now, he was close to losing what little sanity he had left. If she touched him with those soft, sweet hands of hers, he was afraid he would take her too fast and too rough. His hands trembled as he gently looped the restraints around her wrists and tightened them just enough she couldn't break free.

"What....?" Star asked in bewilderment as she watched him tie her hands above her head.

"I am barely hanging on to what little self-control I have. If you touch me...." Jazin explained in a husky tone. "If you touch me, I cannot guarantee what will happen. Let me love you the only way I can right now. It would kill me to lose control and harm you. You are very small and I am not."

Star opened her mouth to protest, but realized he meant it when he said he was holding on by a thread. A light film of sweat beaded his forehead, a muscle ticked furiously in his clenched jaw, and she could feel the slight trembling of his body as he fought for control. After he had secured her wrists, he slid down her body. He kneed her thighs apart so he could kneel between them. He released a shuddering breath before he reached up and ripped the rest of her nightgown off of her. Star sucked in a surprised breath and bent her knees, lifting her ass up off the bed far enough that he could remove the nightgown from under her.

Jazin leaned down running light kisses and tiny nips along the inside of her right thigh. His pulse sped into high speed when she lifted up again, unknowingly opening herself to him in invitation. The heady scent of her arousal burst over his senses pulling a low, guttural growl from him. If he thought his cock was hard enough to break crystals with before, he was now even harder.

He pulled back and stepped off the bed. His hand whipped out, wrapping around Star's firm thigh when she moved to close her legs. His eyes were glued to the moist blond curls that begged for him to feast on her molten core.

"Don't," he growled out in a guttural voice.

Star paused, looking at the intense silver flames that had taken over Jazin's eyes. She gulped at the look of primitive male possession in his face. Slowly, she forced her thigh muscles to relax until her legs fell apart.

She felt powerful, beautiful, desirable as the knowledge that only she could bring a man like Jazin to the point of no return and uncontrollable passion. As that power swept through her, it heightened her own desire for him. Moisture pooled between her legs until she wanted to rub it over him, covering him in her scent and her scent alone.

"Fuck me," she purred, letting her eyelids droop until they were half closed. She spread her legs even further apart. "Claim me."

Jazin closed his eyes and absorbed the softly spoken words while breathing in her heady, erotic scent. He reached for his shirt and ripped it off not bothering with the stays on the front. He kicked off his boots and gritted his teeth as he reached for the front of his pants. He quickly shucked them, kicking them to one side.

His eyes flew open when he heard Star's startled gasp. His cock jerked up and down at her frozen gaze. He fisted his cock and pumped it a few times, hoping to relieve some of the pain but it was useless. Only one thing could relieve the pain and she was tied to his bed – finally.

His curse echoed throughout the room when he watched her tiny, pink tongue dart out to lick her lips while her eyes were glued to the movement of his hand as he gently massaged the hard shaft gripped tightly in his palm. When she did it again, he jerked forward.

"Open your mouth," he demanded hoarsely.

Star never took her eyes off his cock. Instead, she opened her mouth and leaned up as far as she could while still restrained. Jazin slid over her until he was kneeling over her, his hands gripping the headboard in a death grip. His long, thick cock was throbbing so painfully he was afraid he would come before he had a chance to feel her hot lips wrap around him.

He leaned forward a little further, crying out loudly as the tip of his cock slid past her lips into her hot mouth. He pushed in as far as he dared before forcing himself to pull back for fear of choking her. He pushed in and out slowly several times, ignoring her whimper of displeasure each time he pulled back.

He looked down at the erotic sight as his cock slid back and forth. His body shook from the force of trying to hold back his own desire until he could satisfy her at least once before he sought his first climax. He might have had a chance of some restraint if Star hadn't taken matters into her own hands – or mouth – as it were. He was sliding his cock in slowly when Star lifted her legs up behind him, wrapped them under his arms and locked them behind his back, forcing him forward with such force he felt his cock sliding down her throat.

His mind shattered as she allowed him to pull back a short way before she did it again. The feel of his swollen cock being squeezed as she worked her throat muscles literally blew his mind. His hoarse cries grew louder and louder until all he could do was knead the headboard with his fingers as his soul was pulled out of him and into her. He threw his head back and closed his eyes in ecstasy as his own throat muscles moved up and down as he gasped for breath.

* * *

Star swallowed rapidly as Jazin's hot seed spilled down her throat. She might not have ever had sex before, but she had watched a few videos in her life out of curiosity so she knew what he wanted as he watched her lick her lips. And this may have been her first blowjob ever, but there was one thing she was good at and that was sword swallowing thanks to the Amazing Kid Cozack, sword swallower extraordinaire. If the look on his face and the trembling in his body was any indication of her ability, he liked it a lot.

She moaned as he pulled out of her mouth slowly so as not to hurt her. She relaxed her legs and let them fall back to the bed. Jazin had his eyes closed and his chin tucked into his chest as he pulled back from her. Star licked her swollen lips and swallowed as he slid down her body.

"Jazin," she whispered.

"Hush," he said harshly with a shake of his head. "Don't say anything…. not yet."

Star looked down as he continued to move down her body with his eyes closed until he was between her parted legs. He buried his mouth in her hot, moist blond curls. Star gasped as she felt his teeth pierce the soft flesh of her mound. She jerked up, her back bowing as intense pleasure and pain swept through her.

"What?" Star gasped out in surprise as tears stung her eyes.

"You are mine, Star. Only mine," he muttered, releasing her. "Say it."

"I'm yours, Jazin," she repeated as she stared up at the ceiling, watching in the mirrored surface as he tugged on her silky curls.

"How many others have you taken that way?" He asked jealously.

"None," she said with a small smile. "Only you."

Jazin felt intense relief sweep through him. He could hear the truth in her voice. He had never experienced anything like that with any of his other lovers before. None had been able to take his large cock into their mouth the way she had. He had never felt such an intense orgasm before either. It had shaken him to the very core of his soul.

"How many others have you taken here?" He asked hoarsely, sliding his thick finger into her slick vaginal channel.

Star gasped at the unexpected intrusion. "None," she choked out. "Only you."

Jazin pulled back before sliding two of his thick, long fingers deeply into her. He could feel the tightness as he pushed into her. When the tips of his fingers encountered a barrier, it took everything in him not to yell out in triumph. Instead, he continued stroking her until she was sobbing. He nibbled, tasted, and sipped her sweet juices until she flowed like a river swollen from the rains. Only then, did he rise up and align his hard, thick shaft to her hot channel.

"Look at me as I claim you as mine," he demanded in a deep, thick voice. "Look at me, my beautiful Star."

Star opened her dazed eyes to stare up at him. She gasped as he released her wrists with one hand and brought them to his chest. Her eyes widened as he began pushing forward, stretching her. She bit her lip at the sudden discomfort, splaying her hands across his chest and shaking her head as it became more painful.

"Jazin?" She asked in a trembling voice. "I don't think you are going to fit down there."

Jazin clenched his teeth. "I'm sorry for hurting you," he whispered harshly, pulling out a little.

Star's sigh of relief turned to a sharp cry of surprise. Instead of pulling out like she thought he was going to, he wrapped his arms tightly around her and surge forward with one powerful thrust of his hips. His thick cock stretched her, breaking through the barrier and burying deeply inside her. His heavy pants and her muffled sob echoed throughout the room. Star tried to push him off her but he merely held her tighter, holding as still as possible until he felt like she could handle him.

Her shuddering breath almost melted his resolve. He turned his head, kissing away the tears that fell from the corner of her eye. He moved his hips again, rocking slowly back and forth. He almost roared out in relief when he felt her small hands gripping him instead of pushing him away. Another few strokes and she began rocking with him. Her legs rose up to wrap around the back of his.

Jazin clenched his jaw tight as the small body beneath him began to move faster. "Can you wrap your legs around my waist?" He grunted out as the friction sent shafts of pure bliss along his cock, tightening his balls until he felt like he was about to explode again.

Star responded by lifting her legs up and wrapping them around his waist. Both of them shuddered as the movement drove him deeper than he ever thought possible. He fought the tingling at the base of his spine that warned him he was about to climax.

"Faster," Star groaned softly. "Just a little faster."

Jazin closed his eyes, groaning at the exquisite feel of her wrapped around him. He rocked harder and faster until he felt her explode around him, fisting him so firmly that he couldn't pull out of her. His cry mixed with hers as they came together, pulsing in a mind-blowing climax that left them both limp.

"You've killed me," Star murmured after her body stopped shaking. "I think I'm dead. I can't move."

Jazin's low chuckle sounded in her ear. "Give me a minute and I'll revive you," he pulled back enough to press a heated kiss on her lips. "I have never felt this way before," he admitted as he stared down at her. "What you do to me…. I have never felt before."

She reached up and gently laid her hand on his cheek as she saw the vulnerability in his eyes and the uncertainty in his voice. "It will be alright," she whispered. "I've never felt this way before either."

Chapter 5

Jazin reluctantly pulled his arms from around Star's sleeping figure. He groaned silently as he lay looking at the ceiling in frustration. He had taken her over and over last night with a desperation that had shocked him. He would never get enough of her.

Guilt poured through him. He glanced at her beautiful, relaxed face with regret. He planned to tell Star last night that he would be gone for a few weeks, maybe more. He needed to test the weapons defense system he was collaborating on with a trusted friend on one of the remote planets on the edge of the Kassis star system.

His friend, Jarmen, preferred the isolation of the small uninhabited planet he had built his home on to living on Kassis. Jazin recognized the quiet darkness in his friend and respected his desire for privacy. He and Jar met several times a year, sharing stories, experiments, and drinks.

Over the last several months, Jar had put together the defense system Jazin had designed and was testing it on a series of scale model warships. They were ready for the final tests. If the tests were successful, the Kassis warships would be virtually impregnable. No one knew where Jar's hidden base was but Jazin. He would be taking a specially modified fighter to the small planet alone.

Rolling out of the bed, Jazin's eyes softened as Star reached out seeking him in her sleep. He pulled his still warm pillow closer to her and chuckled silently when she sighed and buried her face in it. His heart wrenched at the idea of leaving her now but he had no choice. The Intel on Tai Tek could prove devastating if he was successful at arming the Elpidios with information about the Kassis defenses.

The protection of the power crystals they used and his people came before his own happiness. He could only hope that Star would understand. He also knew she would never let him go alone. That was another reason why he felt the guilt. He was sneaking away like a thief.

A curse froze on his lips as he forced himself away from her side. He quickly showered and packed. He stopped only long enough to brush a soft kiss across Star's forehead and slip a video disk he'd quickly recorded onto the pillow next to her. With one last glance, he walked out of the room.

"You will protect her with your life," Jazin told Armet as he strode down the long corridor and out onto the steps leading out of his House. He paused to look at his Captain of the Guard. "I have claimed her. She is Lady Star Ja Kel Coradon now. Do not let her leave the West House alone."

Armet looked at the determination on his young Lord's face. "I will protect her with my life. Good luck on your mission, my lord," Armet said pressing his fist against his chest in respect.

Jazin glanced back at the house one last time before he nodded his head in acknowledgement. He quickly ran down the last of the steps and disappeared through the garden. He had a mission to complete so he could return to the warm arms of his mate.

If she will have me when I get back, he thought with a grimace knowing full well that Star was not going to be happy when she discovered he had left her behind.

* * *

"I'm going to roast his balls over an open fire," Star growled as she paced back and forth. "I need that cage Madas told me about, the one that hangs over boiling water. I'll put him in it and let him sweat his ass out wondering if I'll come along to claim it," she continued as she stomped back and forth in frustration.

It had been two long, long weeks since she had woken to find herself all alone. Two weeks of watching the video disk where Jazin begged her to forgive him for not telling her he had to leave on a mission. Two weeks of silence, wondering if he was safe. Tears of frustration filled her eyes and she impatiently brushed them away.

"Star, I'm sure he will be alright," River said biting her lower lip as she watched her friend. "Torak hasn't said anything. I'm sure he would have told me if something had happened."

Star stopped and scowled at River. "Are you kidding me? The men here don't tell us women anything! I'm lucky if I can go to the bathroom without Armet or one of his guards being with me," she growled out in frustration. "I've had it! If I had known that Jo was leaving yesterday for Earth, I would have been on that warship with her. I'm done with this! I just want to go home."

River rose up to grip Star's arm. She was beginning to show a little now and had a glow about her. She held Star's arm tightly until Star looked at her.

"You don't really mean that, do you?" River asked looking deeply into Star's eyes. "I don't want to be here alone. If it wasn't for you and Jo...." River's voice faded as tears filled her own eyes. "Damn, now I'm getting emotional."

Star sighed. "No, I don't really mean it. It's just.... I love the big oaf and he treats me like I'm this fragile piece of glass. It is driving me nuts," Star said sitting down on the couch.

River gave her a watery grin. "I know what you mean. I think I butt heads with Torak daily. He thinks I should just be sitting around and planning how the servants should clean the North House. Personally, I could care less." A mischievous grin suddenly curved her lips. "How about we break out of this joint and go explore the city?"

Star's eyes widened in excitement before they dropped to the small rounded bump in River's stomach. "What about booger butt?" She asked, nodding to River.

River laid a protective hand over her stomach before she grinned really big. "He likes high places. I've been taking him up almost daily. How do you think I get here?"

Star's lips formed an 'O'. She giggled with excitement. "I just need to change into something more appropriate."

* * *

Three hours later, Star leaned back in the chair at the small restaurant they had discovered. They had escaped by going out the third floor window to the roof. Long, decorative beams connected the four Houses. It had been a piece of cake to walk them. They had then scaled one of the columns that had the fragrant vines climbing all over it near the South House. Once inside, they simply blended in with a group of visitors leaving.

They had visited the market place where they purchased different types of fruits, breads, and jams and several clothing shops. Star was excited about several sets of pants and shirts she had found. She casually rested her newly purchased boots onto the railing overlooking the crystal clear water slapping up against the seawall.

"Now, this is the life," Star giggled as she took a long drink of the fruity ice drink the waitress had brought her. "I am so glad Jazin has a credit line everywhere. Just mentioning his name is better than having a Visa Black card."

River leaned back and propped her feet up next to Star's. "I agree," she said sleepily. "I love those shirts you bought and those boots you are wearing are gorgeous."

"The man in the shop said yours should be ready in a couple of days," Star said with a yawn.

She hadn't been sleeping well since Jazin had left. Right now, she felt like she could curl up in a happy little ball and doze like a cat in a window box. River's yawn drew a chuckle from her. River looked like she felt. Her friend's eyes were drooping even as she took another sip of her drink.

"What do you think my folks are going to think when Jo tells them what happened to us?" Star asked quietly looking at the sparkles reflecting off the water.

"Knowing your folks, they will welcome Manota, Jazin, and Torak with open arms," River said with a sleepy grin. "They love everyone and everyone loves them."

Star's lips curved into a smile. River was right. Alan and Tami Strauss opened their hearts and their homes to anyone and everyone. Both of them were very active in the community, sharing their skills and love of aerial acrobatics at the local community center and working with disabled children. They were both accomplished photographers as well and worked freelance selling their pictures to magazines and other online sites.

"Lady Star," Armet's harsh voice broke through her musings.

Star groaned out loud in frustration. Busted! He would probably put her in the dungeon until Jazin returned now. River's groan echoed Star's when she heard Dakar's voice.

"Kev's replacement is as bad as he is," River whispered as she put a bright smile on her face. "I have to admit that I love driving him nuts, though."

Star watched as Armet and Dakar wove their way through the tables toward them. Both men had a deep scowl of worry on their face. Star rolled her eyes at River and stood up.

"Hi Armet," Star said cheerfully. "What brings you here?"

Armet's mouth tightened in frustration. When the servant who cleaned Jazin and Star's living area didn't receive an answer to her request for entrance she became concerned and notified the guard. A quick search revealed the apartment was empty. The guard on duty swore that only Lady River had entered and neither she nor Lady Star had left. Armet contacted Dakar and discovered neither he nor any of Torak's guards were aware that Lady River had left the North House. That left one conclusion, they had snuck out.

He and Dakar, along with a small army of North and West House guards, had scoured the city looking for the two women. Their unusual coloring and the fact that they were moderately famous helped in the search. After following their trail of visits to local merchants who had not only been fascinated with the two females, but utterly entranced by their friendliness and unusual beauty, they had finally located them. Armet ground his teeth when he saw them relaxing back, totally oblivious to the fact that a small crowd of onlookers had gathered to see the unusual species that had captured not only the hearts of the royal family but the imagination of the Kassisan people.

"Would you like a drink?" Star asked with a grin. "They make the most incredible fruity drink here. I bet they could even put some liquor in it to help you loosen up a little. You know being all doom and gloom all the time can't be good for your blood pressure," she teased.

"Make that two," River said, tilting her head back and looking at Dakar's tightly controlled face. "Hi Dakar."

"Lady River," Dakar acknowledged stiffly.

River rolled her eyes and looked at Star. "I think we need to request a bottle of the good stuff. Do you think Torak would be upset when that shows up on his credit?" She asked mischievously.

Star's light, husky laughter drew the attention of all the males in the establishment and a frustrated groan out of Armet. He knew the tiny female had no clue as to the effect she had on the Kassisan males. Even he wasn't immune to her delicate looks and husky voice. She was like the small, fragile imaginary creatures told to all Kassisan children when they were little.

Her long, sun kissed hair sparkled when the sun touched it, her rosy cheeks, dancing eyes, and tiny, perfectly proportioned figure pulled at a warrior's need to protect. Her husky voice pulled at the male's need to possess and claim. Armet ground his teeth together as he felt both responses to her.

"My ladies, I think it would be best if we returned to the Royal Houses," Dakar said in a cool voice.

"Lord Torak will not be happy that you left without protection."

River's eyebrow rose at Dakar's tone. "No offense, Dakar, but I happen to be over the age of having to ask permission if I want to go out for a while."

Dakar flushed as River's unusual, dark blue eyes stared at him steadily in challenge. A muscle ticked in his jaw before he bowed his head in respect. River refused to back down. Dakar needed to learn that she wasn't going to be intimidated by him or anyone else. Besides, she wasn't stupid. She had enough blades on her to handle just about anything.

"My lady, I promised Lord Jazin that I would protect you with my life," Armet said quietly, stepping closer to Star. "From now on, if you wish to visit the markets or shops in the city, I will make arrangements for it. I just ask that you not leave the West House without proper protection," he added reluctantly.

Star's mouth twisted in remorse when she noticed the strained look on Armet's face. "I'm not used to asking for permission to do things," she responded with a rueful grin. "I can't promise, but I'll try. I will tell you, and I'll tell Jazin when I see him again, that I will not be kept in a gilded cage."

Armet bowed his head briefly to show he heard the steel behind her words. A reluctant smile tugged at the corner of his mouth. He had heard the rumors that the three females were the prophesied warriors spoken of in a recently discovered temple in the ruins of Karazdin, the ancient city of knowledge.

If he had not fought during the battle several weeks ago and saw the dead warriors in the garden for himself, he would never have believed it possible for females to be warriors. The fact that the two females could also escape the Royal Houses without being seen proved their skills at moving unseen through a highly secured area. A feat an experienced warrior would have difficulty doing.

"I do not believe there is a cage in all the known galaxies that could hold you for long, my lady," Armet admitted reluctantly.

"Armet," Dakar's voice called out. "We need to return immediately."

Star looked at Dakar's face. He had been listening into the com attached to his ear intently for the past several minutes. His eyes had grown colder the longer he listened and his eyes had focused on her face. A feeling of unease rolled through her stomach. Something was wrong. She could feel it as a shiver coursed through her body. Something had happened to....

"Jazin," Star breathed out, looking at Dakar's face intently as she said the name of the man who meant everything to her.

The flicker in his eyes told her the feeling of unease had been correct. Star reached down and grabbed the bags at her feet. River rose immediately, a look of concern on her face as she stared at Star. No words were necessary. River had sensed the same thing she had. Something bad had happened to the man she loved.

Armet reached over and took the bags from Star and River, stepping back so the two women could move ahead of him. Star numbly followed Dakar's lethal figure through the crowded room and out into the street. A transport pulled up and he opened the door.

Neither woman said a word as they quickly slid into it. Star stared blindly out the window as the transport rose and did a U-turn in the middle of the busy street. They wove through the streets at a fast pace heading back to the palace. Star jerked in surprise when she felt River curl her fingers around her cold ones.

"Everything will be alright," River whispered compassionately.

Star opened her mouth before closing it. She nodded once before turning to look back out the window at the blurred images of buildings and people going about their daily life. She saw none of that. The only image she had in mind was of Jazin's beautiful smile as he looked down on her after he had claimed her. A single tear escaped and coursed silently down her cheek. She refused to believe that would be her last image of him.

Chapter 6

The transport slowed as it pulled up in front of the steps to the South House. Dakar slid out quickly once it stopped. He scanned the area carefully before he stepped back far enough for River, Star and Armet to slide out. Armet took Star by the elbow while Dakar escorted River toward the steps leading to the front entrance. Torak and Ajaska were standing at the top, waiting.

Torak immediately descended the steps when he saw River. He drew her into his arms, holding her tightly against him. Ajaska looked sadly down at Star. He opened his huge arms for her without saying a word.

Star shook her head in denial even as she slowly climbed the steps. Her heart beat erratically as she stopped in front of him and looked up. She stared at Ajaska for a brief moment before stepping into his embrace as uncontrollable shivers began coursing through her.

"Please tell me he is okay," she begged in a voice thick with tears. "Please tell me he isn't.... He isn't...." She turned her face into the warm muscular chest and fought unsuccessfully to control the sob that was trying to escape.

Grief pulled at Ajaska as he held the tiny mate of his youngest son in his arms. Pain and sorrow poured through him as he felt her fear and disbelief. He and Torak had just received word that Jazin's fighter had been destroyed while returning from the Uri Spaceport. Initial reports say that it had exploded shortly after leaving the popular refueling station. The unofficial report states the fighter was believed to have been damaged when a short-haul freighter came in too quickly and struck it.

"I'm so sorry, my daughter," Ajaska murmured as he ran his hand over the silky, blond strands. "He did not suffer," Ajaska reassured her even as his eyes closed as pain swept through him.

"NO!" Star's muffled cry of pain and grief poured out from the center of her soul.

Ajaska caught her as she collapsed, sobs tearing at her tiny body until he feared she would harm herself as she shook. He picked her up in his arms and turned to enter the South House, heading towards medical. Star's wretched sobs echoed as he moved through the silent corridors. Torak followed, holding River's weeping figure protectively against his body. His own face twisted with grief as he followed his father.

* * *

Star sat in the chair by the window, staring out at the gardens with unseeing eyes. It had been a little over a week since Ajaska told her that Jazin had been killed. She remembered very little of the first few days. A numbness had settled around her.

She knew what was going on but she was more of a ghost observing everything from the outside instead of being a participant. She didn't remember eating, drinking, or sleeping. She knew who came and who went, but that was all. She didn't respond to anyone;

not even to River who came daily to spend time with her.

"Star, try to drink some of this," River was saying as she held a cup out to her. "It is a broth that will help you keep your strength up."

Star fought down the bile that rose at the smell of the liquid. She turned her head slightly away from the smell. She heard River's sigh and the sound of the cup being set down on the table. In the background, she heard someone knocking on the outer doors. The knocking became more persistent until River finally released a muttered oath and stood up to answer it.

Star heard muffled voices from the other room before footsteps echoed quietly against the tiled floors. She didn't know who had come to visit. She didn't care. She was waiting. For what, she didn't know for sure. Perhaps for the numbness to wear off. Perhaps for someone to say there was a mistake and Jazin hadn't been killed. Perhaps for death so she couldn't feel the mind-numbing pain that was eating away at her. She didn't know and really didn't care. She would sit here and wait.

"Star," River called out softly. "Madas is here to see you."

She didn't respond. She listened as River explained to Madas that she had been unresponsive since the sedative the healer gave her wore off after the first day. Madas asked several questions before asking River if she would mind if she spoke to Star alone.

"I need to check on Torak. He has taken this hard as well," River was saying. "Please let the guard know before you leave. I don't want to leave her alone for too long."

"I promise she will not be left alone," Madas hissed out softly. "Do not give up hope yet, Lady River. There are some things that are yet to be revealed."

River looked inquisitively at Madas for a moment before she nodded. "I'll be back soon, Star," River said quietly as she walked over and knelt next to Star's chair. River squeezed her friend's hand tightly. "I love you, little sister. Never forget that." River rose and nodded tearfully to Madas before quietly leaving.

Madas watched as the slender figure walked out. What she had to say was for the little warrior's ears only. The Gods had sent a message and Madas firmly believed it was time for the little warrior to prove how fierce she could be. Madas looked at the still figure sitting in the chair. The light played with the colors of spun gold in her hair. Her face was still, almost serene. It was as if she was waiting for something. Perhaps she was waiting for Madas.

"Little warrior," Madas hissed quietly. "Your mate needs you."

Star didn't respond, but something told Madas that she was listening. That was all that Madas wanted. Her own mate was being stubborn and refused to believe her. There had only been one other person Madas knew who might believe her wild dream – the person who knew the man responsible for Jazin's supposed death.

"He is not dead. He is a prisoner. It is time to claim your mate before he is truly taken from this life," Madas hissed out in a firm voice filled with confidence and belief. "The Gods have spoken to me. I need you to believe."

Star's head turned and she stared silently into Madas' black eyes for several long minutes. Madas did not look away. She needed the little warrior to believe her – to trust her.

Madas held no animosity that her own mate did not believe in her dreams. He had been raised to believe in logic and facts while Madas had been raised to believe in the spirit of the Gods and the messages they often sent through dreams. Her grandmother had been their clan's spiritual leader and Madas had been taught at a young age to believe and accept the wills of the Gods. Too many times when she was growing up, she had visions that had spared or helped her clan by believing in them.

Her dream several nights ago showed her where to start and who she needed to enlist to help her. The sight of the little warrior standing fierce and proud in the face of battle in the dark fortress, her mate standing at her side had been one of the clearest visions she had ever had.

"How?" Star's raspy voice asked. "How do you know?"

"Look deep inside your heart," Madas said, reaching out a slender clawed finger to touch Star's chest. "What does it tell you?"

Star closed her eyes briefly, focusing inward. What did her heart tell her? She felt the slow, strong, steady beats. There was no way it could beat so strongly, so steady if it was missing. She knew if Jazin had died, then there was no way it could beat the way it did. For if he had died, her heart would have died with him.

"That he is still there. That he can't be gone," Star said huskily as she opened her eyes. A small hope began to warm her from the inside out.

Madas sank into the chair across from Star. "I had a vision about your mate several nights ago. My visions are not to be ignored. My stubborn mate still has difficulty believing them, but they have protected both of us many times. I saw your mate. He is being held a prisoner. He grows weaker each day, but he lives," Madas said confidently.

Star studied the huge female Tearnat's eyes intently. "Where?"

"My vision did not show me where he was but it did give me clues. Clues that someone who is familiar with the man who took him would know. Clues that would help us find him," Madas continued, reaching out to grip Star's hands tightly in her own.

"Who?" Star asked a little louder. "Who would know?"

"I would," Dakar's voice said quietly from behind them.

Star turned her head to stare at the large Kassisan warrior. His face was grim. Dark shadows rested under his eyes and he looked thinner than he had a little over a week ago. Deep lines cut grooves around his mouth and the muscle in his jaw ticked as he held himself under ridged control.

"How? How could you know?" Star asked softly.

"Because I was Tai Tek's Captain of the Guard. It was my job to keep him safe, alive," Dakar answered harshly. "I was undercover. Lord Ajaska suspected Tai Tek was behind the deaths of several councilmen years ago. I was assigned to his House. I pledged total loyalty to him and over time worked my way up to Captain of the Guard."

"Won't he know that you betrayed him?" Star asked, turning so she could look at the face of the man who suddenly appeared darker and more dangerous than she remembered.

Dakar shook his head briefly. "He believes I was killed during the battle. Images of my body, riddled with laser blasts, were sent out. My brother publicly condemned me as a traitor to our people. As far as everyone is concerned, I no longer exist," he explained in an emotionless voice.

"But," Star began shaking her head in confusion. "Wouldn't people recognize you?"

Madas chuckled. "No, they would not. I had a most difficult time in understanding why Dakar was in my dream. I knew Adron very well, having met him many times over the years during meetings with Tai Tek. I did not recognize Dakar as being Adron,

Kel Mul Kar's brother. Only Torak, Manota, and River are aware of his identity."

Star's forehead creased in confusion. How could no one recognize him? She shook her head, trying to clear it. The movement caused her head to spin.

"Drink," Madas encouraged, releasing Star's hands so she could pour a cup of hot tea from the tray sitting on the small end table next to them. Madas pressed the cup into Star's hand. "You must be ready."

"I don't understand," Star confessed, looking back and forth between Dakar's tired face and Madas.

"I underwent facial reconstruction so I wouldn't be recognized," Dakar said, the muscle in his jaw ticking fiercely. "It was the only way without truly dying. When my brother was given the assignment to go with Manota to your home world, Torak asked that I step in to protect Lady River. He felt since I knew Tai Tek and how he thought, I would know better than anyone how to protect his mate from being assassinated should Tai Tek try again. In addition, it gave me more time to – adjust to my new features."

"I approached Dakar," Madas said with a smug smile curling her thin lips. "After a few words, I knew why he was in my dream."

"You tricked me," Dakar muttered with flashing eyes.

"Yes, I did, didn't I?" Madas said with a twinkle in her eyes.

"So what do we do now? Where do you think Jazin is being held?" Star asked anxiously, leaning forward. "When can we leave?"

"We go after your mate is what we do now," Madas said with a chuckle. "Dakar believes he knows where Lord Jazin is being held based on the descriptions from my dream."

"He is being held on Geylur Prime II. I'm sure of it. Tai Tek has a prison base there and the description matches the terrain of the planet," Dakar replied, throwing a dark look at Madas.

"We leave within the hour," Madas grinned. "I have appropriated an elite Tearnat star ship for our journey. It is a gift from a friend of Lord Jazin. It is a prototype that holds much promise, I have been assured. It just needs to be tested."

"Who will be going with us?" Star asked, looking back and forth when Dakar snorted at Madas' use of the word 'appropriated'.

"Just us," Madas said with a hiss of excitement.

Dakar grunted. "We both felt that the fewer people who knew what we up to, the better. The prison is a fortress. I am not even sure how we will be able to get into it, much less get back out."

"I need to see River before we go," Star said looking steadily at Madas. "She has some items I need to borrow."

"Call her but make sure she understands that she must tell no one, including her mate if possible," Madas said rising to her feet. "I will pick up the items you need on my way out and meet you at the Starship."

Star rose as well. She looked at the huge female Tearnat with her heart in her eyes. "You really are very beautiful," Star said, giving into the urge to wrap her arms tightly around the other female. "Thank you for giving me hope."

"It is my pleasure, little warrior," Madas hissed quietly, holding Star tightly against her for a moment before she pulled away to brush Star's long hair back from her face. "I look forward to seeing the female warrior in action. Something tells me your enemies will not know how to handle you."

Star's eyes glittered with determination. "They are going to learn what happens when they mess with my family," she bit out fiercely.

Dakar groaned and shook his head. "You know if Lord Jazin is alive, he is going to kill me for letting you go, don't you? Gril is going to be right next to him helping," he muttered under his breath.

Both women chuckled at the look of resignation on the large Kassisan warrior's face.

Dakar better just make sure he isn't in the way when, not if, they found Jazin alive because I'm going to take out anyone who tries to stand in my way of bringing him home, Star thought as hope welled up inside her.

Chapter 7

Star dropped down onto the ground outside the South House, pausing to make sure she hadn't been seen. She had used a different method than her and River did when they snuck out. This way was a little more challenging, but she had been less likely to be seen or caught. She felt bad about not telling Armet what she was doing. She reminded herself that she said she would *try* to tell him when she decided to go somewhere first, not that she would.

Besides, she thought, trying to console her guilty conscious, *I did leave a note explaining that I couldn't tell him about it beforehand but for him not to worry about me. That I wasn't alone and I knew what I was doing – sort of.*

She stood up and jogged to the end of the building where Dakar said he would have a transport waiting. She breathed out a sigh of relief when she saw it just where he had promised it would be. Star quickly ran over to the waiting vehicle and slid into the back. She turned breathlessly to thank Dakar again for not trying to insist on going without her. The words died on her lips when she saw he was not alone.

"Uh, hi Armet," Star squeaked out, looking into the dark, glowering eyes of Jazin's Captain of the Guard. "Fancy meeting you here," she added with a guilty expression.

"Yes, fancy that," Armet growled out. "You were supposed to let me know if you needed to go somewhere."

Star wiggled uncomfortably in her seat at his accusing glare. Pushing a strand of hair back that had come loose from her braid, she bit her lower lip and snuck a peek at Dakar who was busy maneuvering through traffic. She glanced back at Armet's furious face.

"I did – sort of," she said with a soft plea for understanding in her eyes. "I left you a note."

Armet's face didn't relax. "I do not read your language," he reminded her before turning around and facing forward. "Do you know how to shoot a laser pistol or wield a laser sword?" He asked gruffly.

It took a minute for Star to understand he wasn't going to return her to the palace. "I know how to shoot a gun and use a regular sword back on my planet. I'm assuming it isn't much different," she responded hopefully.

Armet glanced back at her sternly for a moment before he turned back around again. "Never assume anything. Your life and the lives of your comrades rest on your ability to use both. I will work with you on the way to wherever in the God's name we are going," Armet stated coolly.

Armet was startled into silence when he felt a pair of small, delicate arms wrap around his neck from behind. Soft lips caressed his cheek before Star rested her soft one against his in a fierce hug. Armet felt his heart jerk in response to the unexpected embrace.

"Thank you, Armet," Star whispered in his ear before giving him another kiss. "You have no idea how much this means to me. Jazin is my life."

Armet breathed out deeply when the little warrior released him and sat back in her seat. He stared out the window with sightless eyes. It had been so long since he had felt his heart beat in warmth that he was startled to know that it still could. Not since the woman he loved chose another male from his clan.

There was something about these female warriors from another world that got under a male's skin and drew unwanted feelings from him. Perhaps it was their spirit, their grace, or just their joy in the simple things. All that mattered to him was he would live up to his promise to protect her or die trying.

* * *

Dakar pulled the transport through the gates of a nondescript port. Older shuttles and transports were arriving and departing in a maze of organized confusion. Men yelled to one another as they moved huge shipping containers from one loading dock to another. Dakar pulled down the narrow road between the shuttles, slowing down at times to let men and equipment cross before he sped up again. He continued down the long, narrow corridor between the marked pads, traveling towards the very end of the row.

Star sat forward watching everything with wide eyes. There was so much of this world that she didn't know about. In some ways, it wasn't much different from Earth and in others she had a hard time wrapping her head around it. Especially when she saw a shuttle lifting up into the air before disappearing in a burst of light.

"Madas has the star ship secured at the end. She said not to let the looks of it deceive us. It is much better than its exterior appearance," Dakar said skeptically.

"Where are we?" Star asked as she watched a man in a huge machine that looked like the robot from the movie the *Iron Giant* bend over and pick up a container about the size of a large SUV as if it was a toy and walk away with it.

"Loading Dock Port II. This port is primarily used for off-world imports and exports to the mining colonies on the moons and to the Spaceports along the edges of the Kassis star system," Armet explained. "What docking pad is Madas at?"

"One thirty four A," Dakar responded slowing down and parking next to a small metal building.

"You have got to be joking," Armet said in dismay as he got his first look at the older class Tearnat starship Madas had acquired for their mission.

"Isn't it wonderful!" Star exclaimed excitedly. She leaned over the seat between the two warriors who were staring at the dilapidated starship in front of them in horror.

Both men turned to look at Star in disbelief before looking back at the starship. Armet let out a torrent of silent curses when his second look at the starship didn't look any better than the first. He hoped that they didn't get killed just trying to get off the ground.

He was going to have a long conversation with Madas Tal Mod about the difference between a starship and a pile of worthless bolts. He pressed the button to release the door panel and slid out. He looked at Dakar who was slowly getting out of the transport on the other side. The look on the other warrior's face confirmed that he felt the same way.

"I swore I would protect Lady Star with my life," Armet gritted out. "How in the hell am I supposed to do that if I get us both killed without ever leaving the damn planet?"

Dakar studied the ship in dismay. "Perhaps it will look better up close," he murmured in a doubtful voice.

Star climbed out of the back of the transport, anxious to be on their way. She wanted to find Jazin and every second longer it took twisted at her heart to think of what he might be suffering. She reached for the small pack she had brought with her. Walking by Armet, she called out over her shoulder.

"Come on, what are you waiting for?" She asked impatiently as she strode toward where Madas had climbed down the loading ramp and was waiting for them with an amused expression on her face.

"A miracle?" Armet muttered before he grabbed his own bag off of the floor board of the front seat.

"I don't think we could be so lucky," Dakar muttered under his breath following his two companions.

* * *

Madas watched with amusement as the two Kassisan warriors approached. Both had looks of dismay and skepticism on their faces. She knew what they were thinking. It was exactly what she had expected they would.

While the outside did not look very impressive, it was what was inside that counted. She wouldn't tell them that this was the prototype vessel that Lord Jazin had been working on before he was 'killed'. The morning after her dream, the man Lord Jazin had been working with contacted her. Jarmen D'ju introduced himself simply as a friend of Jazin.

He spoke on condition that Madas did not mention his name to anyone. He stated it was better for him to remain anonymous. Jazin had made Jarmen promise if anything happened to him, Jarmen would contact Madas and ask that she help protect his little mate. He told Madas that Jazin had mentioned her and how she had saved the life of his tiny warrior.

Jar listened as Madas told him of her dream before he shared his doubt that Jazin had been on board the fighter when it exploded. He sent her video from the surveillance equipment from the Uri Spaceport. The blurry images show an unconscious Jazin being hauled away while a Tearnat climbed into the fighter and took off. Madas recognized the Tearnat in question. He had been a personal guard to her son, Trolis.

This information affirmed her belief that her dream was indeed a vision from the Gods. D'ju met with her on the outskirts of the Kassisan star system, just past the third planet ring. He knew she would know how to operate the starship. All he needed to do was show her the modifications that had been done to it. Once he was satisfied Madas understood the operating system, he had disappeared, saying he would do what he could to help rescue Jazin when the time came.

"Welcome, little warrior," Madas called out in greeting. She looked at Armet who was coming up toward her with a deep scowl on his face. "I see you have brought company."

Star looked over her shoulder with a frown. "He figured out what was going on somehow and was waiting in the transport for me. I swear his face is going to freeze like that if he doesn't stop scowling at everything all the time."

Madas chuckled. "I believe his expression will change shortly. Come, the sooner we leave, the sooner we arrive at where we are going."

* * *

"Star ship 782.226 clearance granted. Safe journey," the voice of the control tower stated.

Star trembled nervously from where she was strapped into the chair. She had a clear view out of the front viewport. She watched as the ground slowly slipped away, becoming smaller. A burst of power had her jerking back into her seat.

She held onto the hand grips so hard her knuckles turned white. Within seconds, the darkness of deep space surrounded her and she felt herself relaxing again. She heard a mumble of voices over the communications system as the control tower gave them clearance to the jump gate. Armet answered calmly. Before she could let out the breath she was holding all the way, the lights dimmed on the inside of the starship while outside colors flared as the ship picked up speed as it entered the first jump gate.

"Oh yeah, now this is smooth," Dakar said with a grin of appreciation on his face. "Madas, I know the Tearnats don't have a ship like this. Where in the hell did you get it?"

Madas chuckled as she relaxed back. She was a good pilot, but she was nowhere as good as the two warriors in front of her. She had done her homework last night after she had worn her mate out. She knew Gril was going to come after her once he realized what she was up to. He was very protective of her. She often got amused at his need to protect her and his possessive behavior. She enjoyed keeping him on his claws. He was an excellent lover, but when he was outraged with her over something, a shiver of delight flared in Madas as she thought of her mate's reaction to this little adventure.

Yes, it will be worth his anger when I return, Madas thought with a small smile.

"It is a gift from a friend of Lord Jazin. He confirmed that Jazin was not on board the fighter when it exploded. A traitor to the Tearnat was the victim. Tai Tek is behind your prince's disappearance," Madas assured both men.

"How do you know for sure this 'supposed' friend is on our side?" Star asked, worrying her bottom lip. "What if it is a trap?"

Madas reached over and gently unclenched Star's fisted hand and held it tenderly in her larger one. "Trust me, little warrior. I would not lead you into a trap. The warrior who gave me this starship is to be trusted. He knew things about you that only your mate could have told him. Things that he would not have shared with an enemy, not even under torture."

Star's eyes filled with tears at the thought of Jazin telling someone else about her. "Like what?" She asked in an unsteady voice.

Madas reached over and picked up a strand of golden hair, letting it run over her slender fingers. "Like how your hair is the color of the sun touched with gold on a clear day and how beautiful, strong, and brave you were against those much larger and fiercer than you. He spoke of your courage and loyalty. But most of all, he spoke of his respect and love for you."

A single tear slid down Star's face. For a moment, it was as if she could feel Jazin brushing it away with a tender kiss. She closed her eyes and pulled an image of him into her mind. She gripped Madas hand tightly, wishing with everything in her that it was Jazin holding it. She breathed deeply before she opened her eyes and stared at her friend.

"He is alive," Star whispered. "I can feel him. In here," she said, touching her chest over her heart. "I can feel him calling to me."

Madas nodded. "He is alive, little warrior. He has much to live for."

Chapter 8

Pain racked Jazin's body where he hung from the wall. He leaned forward, resting his head against the hard stone trying to relieve the pressure on his shoulders. Exhaustion beat at him, but he refused to give into it. He let his mind turn instead to Star.

Over the past week or more since he had been captured, the picture of her face staring up at him was the only thing that kept him from going insane. Tai Tek had personally been seeing to his torture. The numerous cuts, bruises, and burns attested to the former councilman's desire to take his frustration out on Jazin. His methods of trying to extract information from him were becoming more brutal.

His latest ploy was to see how long Jazin could stand upright without dislocating both of his shoulders. His arms were chained out to the side and only his standing, gripping the chains tightly in his fists prevented the heavy weights attached to the ends from pulling his arms out of their sockets. He had been like this for the past six hours or more.

Every once in a while, Tai Tek would come in with a whip and viciously strike him over and over, leaving his back a bloody mass of torn flesh. Jazin refused to give Tai Tek the satisfaction of seeing him in pain. He stared at the wall with a cold, impassive face as blow after blow ripped at his flesh.

His mind turned to Star and the memories of how her gentle hands had caressed him the night before he left. Tai Tek had left him several hours ago with a curse that he would make sure Jazin talked when he returned or else.

Jazin knew he wouldn't last much longer. Not only because his strength was waning but because Tai Tek was growing increasingly more desperate. That desperation was leading to more brutal blows. It was only a matter of time before one of them lead to his death. He would never reveal the information that Tai Tek wanted. He would die first.

He stared at the ceiling of his prison and fought back a wave of grief at the idea of never seeing his mate again. If he could have just one more moment with her, he would tell her that just the short time they had together brought him more joy than anything else in his life. His eyes burned but he refused to let the tears of grief to form. He would only think of Star's beauty. He would only relive the times when her fierce spirit woke a need inside him that he never thought to have.

"I love you, my fierce little warrior," Jazin whispered into the darkness of his prison cell. "More than anything, I wish I could tell you one last time how much."

His head dropped down to rest on his chest as exhaustion pulled at the chains holding him. Perhaps he should let death take him. As long as he had his memories of Star, he would not die alone. He would seek her out in another lifetime. He would always look for her, no matter where the Gods sent him. She was his soul mate – forever.

Jazin didn't bother raising his head up when the door to his cell creaked open. He mentally tried to prepare himself for another beating. He pulled even further into his tired mind, seeking shelter as he felt first one wrist than the other being unchained. He had no idea what new torture Tai Tek had for him, but he would die a warrior. He forced his head up as he was turned around and stared straight into the eyes of his tormentor.

A frown creased his forehead as he saw a set of familiar eyes, instead. The dark, glowing amber eyes met his for a brief moment before turning away. As his strained arms fell to his side weakly, the huge figure of the male in front of him lowered him down to the cold, stone floor gently.

"Your warrior mate is coming for you," the voice whispered hoarsely. "Stay alive. She is not alone, and neither are you."

Jazin let his head rest weakly against the floor. He didn't know if the voice or the figure had been a figment of his imagination. Perhaps this was one of Tai Tek's tricks to torture his mind as well as his body by giving him hope. He rolled weakly over and looked around the dimly lit cell through blurry eyes. He was alone. Rolling over again, he curled up as far as his battered body would let him to preserve his body heat against the cold of the rock cell he was locked in.

His mind drifted back to the first time he saw Star. Everything became fuzzy as his body and mind began shutting down in exhaustion. He reached up with trembling fingers to touch the faint scar on his cheek where Progit had cut him. All he could think of was when Star had touched him for the first time. Her tender touch as she gently wiped the blood away and her softly spoken words. His head turned slightly when he thought he felt her gentle fingers against his cheek for a moment.

"You are safe now," her husky voice whispered through the lonely cell.

"I know," he whispered back. "As long as I have you in my heart, I'll always be safe," he responded to the ghost in his mind as darkness settled over him.

* * *

Star jerked awake from the dream she was having. She sat up trembling, her hand covered her mouth as silent tears flowed down her cheeks. She had seen him. She had seen Jazin. He had been in a dark cell chained to a wall at first before she saw him again lying curled up. His body was covered in welts, bruises, and cuts from being beaten.

She pushed the covers on the narrow bed back and slid her feet into the soft brown leather boots. Pushing her hair back impatiently, she straightened her top before walking over to the small closet-size cleansing room. She stood looking at her pale reflection. Her eyes seemed too large for her face and were slightly red from crying in her sleep. She could have sworn she had touched him. She could feel his skin under her fingertips as she caressed his cheek.

She looked down at her fingers and was surprised to see a small trace of red on the tips. Her hands trembled as she raised them up to the dim lighting above the small mirror. Small streaks of dried blood were barely visible on the tips but they were there. Star looked back at the reflection in the mirror trying to see if she had scratched herself in her sleep. She looked frantically, ripping open her shirt and checking her arms, chest, face, and stomach for any sign of injury that could explain the blood on her fingers.

Nothing, she thought. *No scratches, not cuts, no marks except* …. Her eyes rose to look in the mirror again in disbelief. She had been with him. She knew it. She had told him he was safe now.

Star fumbled with refastening her shirt. She quickly braided her hair, brushed her teeth, and washed her face. Her eyes were glued to the faint trail of red as she washed her hands before it disappeared. Her face hardened into a frozen mask of determination. She was going to bring him home. Her eyes glittered with fury as she stared into the mirror one last time before she turned to find Madas. She was going to bring him home and she was going to kill the man who had hurt him. No one messed with her family and lived, no one!

* * *

Dakar set a cup of steaming tea down in front of Star before he moved around the narrow table they were using as a conference table to sit on the other side. Madas let her tongue taste the brew before she smiled in pleasure and took a deep sip of it. Armet pushed into the room late. He had set the auto-pilot and wanted to double check some of the weapons systems before joining them.

"This is what we are facing. We need to not only break into this fortress but then try to get out of it in one piece," Dakar said pulling up a three-dimensional map of Tai Tek's prison fortress. "There are four levels in all. Three above ground and one below. The cells are below ground, of course. Look at these towers. There are six of them. Each has a high power laser cannon capable of bringing down any size fighter. In addition, there are smaller automated laser cannons that can be controlled from this center building. They are set to automatically fire at anything that shows a heat signature. You would see what I mean if you could walk around the perimeter of the fortress," Dakar said in disgust. "It is littered with the remains of any creature unfortunate enough to wander into the firing range. Truthfully, I don't think there is any way to get into the fortress alive."

Star stared at the structure in front of her. Her eyes following the lines of the fortress as Dakar showed it from different angles and explaining the materials used to build it. Her eyes kept going back to the long, thin cable that extended from the mountainside where the fortress was built into the main control rooms in the center of the grounds.

"What about from above?" She asked hesitantly. "Are the cannons aimed for anything coming from above the fortress?"

"Of course, they are set to fire on any incoming vehicle," Dakar said, pointing to a series of cannons pointed upward.

"Yes, but what about from here?" Star asked, pointing to the narrow aqueduct system that came out of the mountain and the cable attached to right below it to the center building. "What about if someone were to go through the access tunnel at the top of the mountain? They could make their way to this release duct. Would the cannons detect someone coming across the wire from where it is connected here to the control tower?"

Armet leaned forward studying the areas Star was asking about. He shook his head. "There is no way to do that. The vents are too small. They can't be more than two feet in diameter. Even if Dakar or I could fit through there we wouldn't be able to cross the cable. There is a security field set up that stops about a foot under the wire."

"But, if someone was able to make their way through the vent, cross the cable to the control tower, and take out the control room, it would allow others to breach the fortress, right?" Star insisted looking at the wire that ran down where it attached just outside an access door to the control room. It was a left over from the building stage and had probably been left as an afterthought for maintenance.

"IF someone could squeeze through the narrow tube AND cross the wire without triggering the alarms, then yes, I guess it is possible to bring the system down long enough to get additional support inside," Armet said reluctantly as he looked with growing unease at Star who was smiling.

"Then, we know how we will get in. Dakar, I will need you and Armet. Jazin is hurt, and I'm not big enough or strong enough to carry him out. You know the inside of the prison, Dakar. You will know where they are likely to be keeping him. Madas, you will have to pilot the starship," Star said, looking excitedly from one frowning face to another to the last which had a grin on it.

"No, little warrior. I will go with Dakar. Armet is the better pilot. Once their defenses are down and we have Lord Jazin, we will have to be able to leave quickly. The starship is capable of landing in this area," Madas said, pointing to a larger area used for training exercises. "I am a fair pilot, but we need an excellent pilot who can come in fast and leave just as quickly."

Star looked at Madas for a moment before looking at Armet's tight face of disapproval. "She's right. She is strong enough to help carry Jazin."

"No," Armet said harshly, looking at the little human female in frustration, even though he knew she was right. "I promised I would keep you safe."

"And you will," Star interrupted, leaning forward to place her hand on top of his. "By getting us out of there safely. I can do this. You've been working with me and I have a few tricks up my sleeve. Please, Armet," she whispered looking into his eyes with determination. "I can't lose him. I love him and I can't lose him, not again."

The muscle ticked in Armet's jaw as he stared into Star's bright, light blue eyes. His eyes moved to Dakar who was sitting back with a grim expression on his face as well. Their eyes collided with the unspoken message that neither liked the plan but they both accepted it was the only way. His eyes finally traveled to the huge female Tearnat who was sitting back with a smug look on her face and a twinkle in her eye. If he didn't know better, he would swear she knew something that neither he nor Dakar were aware of and that just made the muscle tick faster.

"I want to go over some strategies with you before we drop your ass off," Armet said in a low, gruff voice. "You better not get yourself captured or killed. I swear, if anything happens to you I will personally take that damn place apart stone by stone. You are just too damn small and delicate to be doing this," he added under his breath.

Star squeezed the hand she was still holding. "I may be small and I may not be as strong as a Tearnat female, or even a Kassisan one, but I have a strength built on love and determination to bring my mate home. I won't fail and I won't die. I have too much to live for," she declared in a quiet, passionate voice. "Believe in me."

"I do," Madas said, reaching out and laying her slender, green hand on top of Star and Armet's hands.

"Oh Gods," Dakar muttered in a dark voice before laying his hand on top of Madas' hand. "I do too. It is so crazy it just might work," he said with a disbelieving chuckle as he watched the image of the fortress circle slowly in the center of the table.

Chapter 9

Star and Madas giggled like a couple of high school girls at a classic car show with their boyfriends as they listened to Dakar and Armet oohing and awing about all the modifications to the starship. One of the defense system upgrades to it was the ability to deflect any type of radar from detecting it. The second upgrade was the new engine design.

Jazin was able to develop an engine that was not only more powerful but also did not release a heat signature. This made it virtually impossible to detect and track. The last upgrade was the most important as it would give them the advantage they would need when Armet came in hot and fast – it had a cloaking device.

"Guys aren't much different when it comes to their toys," Star said as she watched the two men talking excitedly as they discovered another feature they had missed earlier when they were exploring.

"Gril is the same," Madas replied with a shake of her head. "He understands the things he can touch, not the things he cannot," she added softly. "I miss him. I am not used to being away from him for this long."

Star reached over and touched her friend's hand. "Is he going to be upset with you?" She asked, biting her lip in guilt.

Madas chuckled and looked at Star with a mischievous look in her eyes. "I hope so. I like it when he is upset."

Star's eyes widened at her friend's innuendo and she blushed, drawing another chuckle from Madas. "I never thanked you for giving me hope," Star murmured as tears formed in her eyes.

If Madas hadn't come to her, she would have never known what had truly happened to Jazin. He would have been left to die at the hands of Tai Tek and no one would have been any the wiser. He might still die, but Star refused to believe that she could come so close to finding him and he not survive. He had to be alive. She touched her chest, feeling the steady beating of her heart and drew strength from the thought that it still beat because his did as well.

"It was the Gods who gave you the guidance that you needed. I am merely their messenger. Plus, I was ready for an adventure. It is not fair that Gril gets to have all the excitement. It will do him well to remember that I am a warrior as well. Your mate will learn that about you too, little warrior. You were right when you said you might be smaller and more delicate but you have a strength inside you that one does not often see, even in the biggest, fiercest warrior. Your heart will guide you in your journey," Madas stated confidently. "I consider myself fortunate to call you my friend and to stand beside you in battle."

Star rose up out of her seat and flung her arms around Madas' neck, holding on tight as she hugged her friend. Madas was truly the first person, or species, besides Walter that made Star feel like she was just as big and strong as everyone else. She buried her face in Madas' soft neck before leaning back and giving her unusual friend a kiss on her silky cheek.

"Thank you again," Star whispered, looking up into Madas' dark eyes. "I'm glad you are my friend."

"It is my pleasure, little warrior, it is my pleasure," Madas replied, smoothing a strand of soft blond hair back behind Star's ear.

..*

"Focus, Star," Armet growled out as he and Dakar circled her with a set of training laser swords. "If you are found, you will more than likely have more than one warrior coming at you. You need to know how to defend yourself."

"Yes, but why do I have to only defend myself this way?" Star asked in frustration as she shook off another sting from where Armet's sword had struck her shoulder.

"We are trying to teach you how to defend yourself against one or more aggressors at the same time," Dakar bit out. "You would be dead half a dozen times by now," he snarled. He glanced at Armet in frustration. "There is no way we can let her do this, Armet! She is going to get herself caught or killed. Either way, she poses more of a danger to Jazin. If she is captured, they will use her to get whatever information they want out of him. If she is dead, Jazin will soon follow."

Star turned and attacked Dakar. *To hell with them,* she thought savagely.

She didn't have time to learn how to fight the way the warriors were trained to fight. They spent years learning. She had a few days! Well, she would show them some of the ways a circus performer learned.

More than once, the performers had been on the receiving end to a few rowdy townspeople who thought it would be fun to pick on the 'freaks'. Even Walter knew a thing or two about how to fight. It wasn't always fair and it wasn't always fancy, but it worked.

Star used her strength, her agility, and her natural athletic ability to guide her through strike after strike. When the men started fighting back in self-defense, she used the layout of the room to help her. Running at Dakar, she ducked down, bringing the laser sword across the front of his legs. As he fell, she did a one handed flip over him slicing the sword across his neck before flipping gracefully in an arch and rolling behind Armet and slicing him twice, once across the back of his knees and the other across the back of his neck.

Star rose as both men gasped at the stinging shock from the laser sword. "I will be going and I will get Jazin. No one, and I mean no one, is going to stop me," she hissed out coldly.

Armet rolled onto his back and grasped the back of his neck which was burning. "You have your sword turned up to full power, don't you?" He croaked out. "Because I have to tell you, this hurts like a...." He stopped and looked at Madas who was laughing at him and Dakar.

"I told you. She is the warrior from the Prophesy and not to underestimate her," Madas said smugly. "I was the one who turned the power up. You both needed to know what she was capable of."

Star looked down in dismay. The two warriors' faces were twisted in pain. "Did I really hurt them?" She asked, looking at Madas in question.

"No, they will be fine in a few minutes. You just showed them that there are many ways a warrior can fight. Come, let us go through the items you will need. I have made some explosives for you. One of them is unique to the Tearnat. The powder in them will knock everyone out for several hours. It is important that you do not breathe it in. I want to go over with you how it works," Madas said as she drew Star away by the arm. She turned as she reached the door to cast one last look at the men who were now sitting up. "Now, I will show her how to fight like a Tearnat."

"Great," Armet muttered as he rubbed the back of his neck again. "Just great."

* * *

"These are small but they are very potent," Madas said as she showed Star several small, round balls that looked like they were made out of clay. "If you throw them, they will break and a dust cloud will be released. The dust is pollen from a plant found near my village. It is used mostly when someone is injured and needs to be put to sleep so they can be healed. It can also be used to help incapacitate our enemy without killing them. The only thing that can protect you is this," Madas said, pulling a small woven mask of plant fibers. "This is a natural absorbent for the pollen. If a warrior tries to use a filtering mask it will not work, the pollen is so fine, it still finds its way through the masks. It might not stop them totally but it will slow them down."

"I look like a ninja," Star said with a grin as she put the woven mask on. "It is so light it's like not having anything on!" She exclaimed in surprise.

Madas chuckled. "That is why we like it. Otherwise, it would restrict our breathing."

"Here are the weapons you had me pick up from Lady River," Madas said, pulling out the small crossbow that Star excelled at using, in addition, to several small throwing knives. "She said she would give us a one day head start before she told her mate. She is not aware that this starship is faster than even the Kassisan warships. Still, I am sure they will be here to support us by the time we have need of it."

Star looked at Madas puzzled. "Did you tell them where we were going?"

"No, but between Gril, Ajaska, and Torak I am sure they will be able to discover our location," Madas assured Star. "Do not worry, little warrior. I would not risk your mate. I suspect if Tai Tek feels there is a possibility that his prison base had been discovered, he would have already killed Lord Jazin. It is better that only a small group is aware of what is happening until he is safe."

Star nodded in agreement. "I hope you are right." She looked at the small three-dimensional image of the fortress and sighed. "I hope you are right," she repeated quietly.

* * *

Jarmen lowered his head as he walked by a small group of guards. The small device attached to his cloak rendered him invisible to the eye for the most part. The only thing that could still be seen were his glowing eyes, a left over from his days in the Mendes Research labs where he had been created. He pressed along the side, sucking in his breath when one of the guards staggered slightly, almost running into him. He might be invisible but he could still be felt.

It had taken him longer than he expected to gain entrance to the prison. He had landed his small transport several kilometers away and hiked closer to the fortress four days before. He had camped just outside the dead zone, trying to figure out how he was going to get in.

His luck changed on the morning of the fifth day when a small group of guards had driven a series of transports out through the entrance to discard waste in a nearby ravine that had broken open probably a thousand years ago. He waited until the last one backed up before grabbing a maintenance grip and holding on for the journey back to the prison.

He had searched section after section, level after level for where his friend was being held. He had almost given up until he rounded a corner and almost collided with Tai Tek. If one of the guards hadn't called his attention at the last minute, Jarmen would now probably be enjoying the bottom of the deep ravine with the trash.

He had followed Tai Tek for almost an hour before the traitorous councilman finally made his way down to Jazin. Jarmen closed his eyes and cursed silently as his friend was tortured. There was nothing he could do to prevent it. He had been unable to follow Tai Tek into the room because of the number of guards standing in the way.

The coward never went anywhere with less than twenty men surrounding him. It was only after he left that Jarmen was able to sneak into the cell and release his friend. He regretted he could not do more.

He had slipped a dissolvable pain patch on Jazin, but he could do nothing else until the huge Tearnat arrived with Torak's and Ajaska's forces. He had been shocked when the female mate of the Tearnat Leader had not only recognized him, but told him things she shouldn't have known. It was only her insistent demands that Jazin hadn't been killed that had finally gotten through to him.

He had done a little research and discovered the real video surveillance from the Uri Spaceport docking bay that Jazin had refueled at but had been skeptical until he had shown the video to the female.

Once he saw the evidence for himself, he had contacted the female again and given her the prototype he and Jazin had been working on so it could be used to rescue Jazin. He knew only a small, stealthy team of warriors would be able to save Jazin before he could be executed. In the meantime, he would do what he could to help his friend survive until the warriors arrived.

Jarmen lifted his head and walked silently back down to the prison cell holding Jazin. His thoughts turned to a time when it had been him in such a place. His torture had been different. His tormentors had been the scientists experimenting with ways to create the ultimate warrior. They had succeeded to a certain extent. His body and mind were that of the perfect warrior. He could move, think, and kill faster than any other. The one thing they failed to do, though, was eliminate his conscience, no matter how many times they tried.

Jazin had discovered information about the illegal research facility from a drunken guard on leave. The man had a video chip of some of the experiments. He swore it was the only thing that kept him alive.

The man told Jazin that other guards who decided to leave the research facility would disappear, only to later become one of the casualties of the researchers' experiments. He was determined he wouldn't end up becoming a monster like what the doctors had created or dead like some of the other guards he had known. He had shown Jazin the disk.

Jarmen had been the monster they had been working on at the time. A fortnight later, Jazin and a small group of his elite guards had entered the facility determined to shut it down. The battle had been brief, but deadly.

The researchers had ordered all experiments to be terminated immediately if the facility was breached.

Jarmen wasn't sure how many there had actually been, but he knew he was one of the few to have survived from the records he had been able to hack into before the files were destroyed. He had been severely wounded by the guards.

It had been Jazin who had saved him and taken him to the small, isolated planet he now called his own. He had built a home and research lab of his own and only communicated with the young Kassisan prince who kept his existence a secret. He owed Jazin his life and more.

Jarmen had breathed a sigh of relief that Tai Tek had been called away. It would appear the elusive group of alien warriors he was trying to deal with wanted to meet with him and see what he had to offer in person. Jarmen could only hope they would take one look at the councilman and slit his throat, but he didn't hold too much hope for that simple of a solution. Still, this would give Jazin a day or two to recover before he was subjected to more torture.

Jarmen had weakened several links in the chain to make it appear the links gave out from the weights attached and not through the help of someone. He did not want to give the bastard any more warning of the impending invasion than necessary. He opened the door to Jazin's prison cell, stepped in and shut it quietly behind him.

"Either an apparition with glowing amber eyes just walked into my cell or the Gods have sent me a savior," a hoarse whisper sounded in the darkness.

Jarmen grinned and lifted the cloak from his head. His dark amber eyes glowed with an eerie light in the darkness. "Neither, my friend. Just a monster to keep you company."

Jazin's dry chuckle hurt so much he drew in a breath until the pain faded. "Don't make me laugh, Jar. It hurts too damn much."

Jarmen moved silently closer to where Jazin was sitting up against the back wall. He held out a small container of water and a power vitamin. He turned and sank down on the cold floor next to his friend. He didn't say anything for several minutes while Jazin drank the water and took the small capsule.

"So, what's the plan? How did you know where I was?" Jazin asked in a slightly stronger voice. "And do you have any more pain patches? I hurt so bad I can hardly think."

Jarmen looked at the torn flesh on his friend's shoulder and felt bad he couldn't have snuck a regen bed or something in. Instead, he pulled several patches out of his pocket and handed them to Jazin who placed one on his neck with a sigh of relief. Jarmen watched as the tension slowly ebbed out of Jazin's face as the medicine took the edge off.

"I was contacted by a friend of yours. She told me that you lived and needed help," Jar answered in a rusty voice.

Jazin's head jerked up and he stared at his quiet friend intently. "Who?" He demanded in a harsh whisper.

"A female named Madas Tal Mod. She said she had a dream," Jar said, handing Jazin an energy bar. "Eat. You will need your strength. She said she is bringing the fiercest warrior in Kassis to save you."

"The fiercest warrior in Kassis?" Jazin said with a frown of confusion. "Torak or my father?"

"I do not know. She just said the fiercest warrior in Kassis. She said the Gods sent the warrior to help you," Jarmen said resting his head back and looking around the ragged rocky surface. "My prison was bad but at least it had a cleansing room and bed," he commented in reflection.

The energy bar hovered halfway to Jazin's suddenly dry mouth. His throat closed as Jarmen's words replayed in his mind over and over. The warrior sent by the Gods. The fiercest warrior in Kassis - Star.

His hand fell weakly to his side. "Stop them. Tell them to leave me here. Contact them and tell them whatever you have to but make sure they do…. not…. come…. here!" Jazin bit out savagely. "Now! Before it is too late."

Jarmen turned to look at Jazin puzzled. "It is already too late. I have been monitoring the starship we modified. They are not only on the surface of the planet, but at least three of them have disembarked from it. I do not know their location at this moment. They do not have a communications device activated."

"Damn you," Jazin cursed trying to stand weakly. "You have to find her. You have to stop her before she gets herself captured or killed."

"Who?" Jarmen asked puzzled.

The huge Tearnat looked more than capable of protecting herself, Jarmen thought in confusion. He rose and grabbed hold of Jazin's arm when he staggered drunkenly.

"Star!" Jazin hissed in frustration and fear. "My mate! Star is the warrior Madas was talking about, not my brother, father, or warriors. She is sending Star in. I'm going to kill that lizard if anything happens to my mate," he vowed, shaking off Jarmen's hand as he tried to make his way to the door.

He had only walked a couple of steps before his legs gave out on him and he sank to his knees. His fists pounded weakly into the cold, hard floor in rage and helplessness. He couldn't even walk much less fight, how was he supposed to stop his mate from trying to rescue him. It was a suicide mission.

"I will do what I can," Jarmen said helping Jazin back up and gently settling him back against the wall.

"I won't last another beating," Jazin said in a tired, dead voice. "It is better for her to leave me. I can't even walk. There is no way I can make it out of here without getting her killed."

"You are not alone. With help, we will get you out," Jarmen said stubbornly. "You made me believe in you. Now it is time for you to believe in me," the normally calm voice sounded harsher, gruffer than Jazin had ever heard it before.

"I can't lose her," Jazin said quietly. "If Tai Tek gets his hands on her, I would give him anything he wanted. Even then, he would still kill her. You have to promise me....," he said, swallowing the bile that rose in his throat. "You have to promise me that you will protect her with your life and," he paused again as his throat tightened in grief. "You have to promise if she is captured, you will kill her swiftly before Tai Tek can harm her. I won't let him torture her."

Jarmen frowned as he watched the emotions flickering over Jazin's face. "You would have me kill your mate if she is captured?" He asked in a tight voice.

"Yes," Jazin responded softly. "You've read the reports of what Tai Tek has done to other females. I... won't let that happen to my Star."

Jarmen's mind brought up the reports he had downloaded from Tai Tek's personal files. That was another thing they had worked on this last visit. It had taken Jarmen a while, but he had finally been able to hack into Tai Tek's private accounts to help locate him and determine what he was up to. In those files were records of the hideous things the ex-councilman had done to some of the women in his House.

"I promise," Jarmen said reluctantly. "I will not let your mate suffer."

"Thank you," Jazin said, staring blindly up at the ceiling. "Please keep her safe," he whispered on a quiet prayer.

Chapter 10

Star leaned forward and wiped the sweat beading on her forehead away against her sleeve as she balanced on the narrow ledge she had stopped at to rest for a moment. She looked up at the side of the cliff they were scaling.

They were almost to the top, thank goodness. They had landed a short distance away not wanting to take a chance of being seen disembarking from the starship. It might be invisible to the eye, but they were not.

She could tell Armet had fought a fierce battle with himself before he gruffly told her she better not get hurt or he was going to personally whip her ass. He had spoken quietly at length with Dakar before he had glanced her way one more time before closing the landing platform door. She and Madas had stood off to one side near a small cluster of rocks while the two men hashed out whatever was bothering them.

Star had been a nervous wreck while Madas had just watched the exchange with a small grin on her thin lips. "They will learn not to doubt you, little warrior," Madas said humorously.

"Yeah, well, I think I have enough doubt for all of us," Star muttered as she looked down at her trembling hands.

Madas tilted her head to one side and looked carefully at her little friend. "Do you doubt you can get through the vent?"

Star frowned and shook her head. "Of course not," she scowled.

"Then you doubt you can cross the wire," Madas said.

"That will be a piece of cake," Star scoffed, folding her arms across her chest and glaring at her friend.

"Then you doubt that Jazin can be rescued," Madas suggested calmly.

Star's frown turned to blazing rage and defiance. "No," she growled, letting her arms fall to her side where her fists clenched. "I am going to bring him home no matter what!"

"Then what is there to doubt?" Madas asked gently.

Star opened her mouth and then closed it. Her eyes gleamed with amusement when she realized Madas had been tricking her out of her fear and insecurities; just like Walter used to do all the time. Her friend was one very, very smart lady.

Star chuckled softly. "Do you do this to Gril?" She asked with a small grin.

"All the time," Madas responded lightly. "Come, let us begin our climb. If you need help, ask. I am a very, very good climber."

Over two hours later, Star stared up in envy at the way Madas used her front claws as well as her tail to climb. She could appreciate her friend's offer to help, but she felt a sense of satisfaction at being able to hold her own. She looked down to see how Dakar was doing. She could see the glisten of sweat on his face and shoulders as he climbed just to the left of her. He glanced up and stared at her for a moment before he nodded to let her know he was doing alright.

"Are you doing well?" Dakar called up softly.

Star nodded silently to show she heard him and that she was fine before she turned her attention back to the next and final climb to the top. She reached over, feeling for a good grip. She felt along the narrow edge, making sure she could hold onto it before pulling herself up.

She was just getting ready to reach for the next hand hold when she heard Madas' voice call out in warning. Star had just enough time to see Madas jump to a small ledge as several smaller rocks broke loose. What caught her attention was the large boulder that wobbled precariously before shifting down ever so slightly. Star stared at it for a fraction of a second before she realized that she had to move – and move fast. She called out to Dakar in fear as the boulder shifted a little more.

"Go," he yelled out. "I'm clear of it."

Star looked trying to see where she could go even as more rocks fell, biting into her shoulders and choking her with dust. About four feet from her was a small outcrop. The problem was there was no foothold as the rock wall curved too far under it.

If she was able to jump to it, she would be dependent on just the grip she had with her hands. Madas' harsh hiss echoed loudly as the boulder shifted again and began moving slowly at first then faster. Star had no choice.

It was either try for the outcropping or fall to her death. Taking a deep breath, she focused on the ledge imagining it was a bar being swung out for her to catch. As both Madas and Dakar's cries of horror resonated around her, she pulled the image to her and jumped. She felt the strength in her legs as the adrenaline flowed giving her the extra she needed to reach out and grip the rocky surface. Her left hand slipped, but her right hand held until she found herself hanging almost sixty meters in the air by one hand.

"Gods, no!" Dakar cried out harshly when he saw Star's tiny body dangling precariously.

Madas own strangled cry mixed with his. "Hold on, little warrior," she called down frantically, trying to find a safe way back down.

"I'm fine," Star called out as she swung her left hand up and gripped the rocky ledge.

Using just her upper body strength, she pulled herself up until she was able to get her foot onto the ledge. Balancing on the tips of her toes, she swiveled around on the narrow ledge and looked up at Madas with a grin. Her heart was pounding like crazy, but she felt more alive than she had since the time she had done her first solo trapeze act.

Dakar's oaths echoed as he began climbing again until he was almost level with her. His dark face promised Star he was not as excited about her little stunt as she had been. She raised her eyebrow at him before turning back around and studying the rock face again.

The boulder incident turned out to be a blessing. She saw it would actually be easier to climb up from where she was at now than from where she had been before. Star looked at the incident as a simple test by the Gods, as Madas would say, to see if she was strong enough for what lay ahead of her.

I'm not only strong enough, she thought fiercely, *just try to stop me.* Gods or no Gods, she was going after her mate.

A small part wondered if this was similar to what Gril had to do when he went to save Madas. Maybe that was why Madas was so confident in Star's ability. She knew what it was like to have a mate who would go through anything to save the one meant for them.

Twenty minutes later, Star reached up and gripped the two hands reaching down for her; one was a dark green and the other a dark tan. She chuckled when they lifted her up so high she was over a foot higher than the top of the rocky ground. She looked at the two much larger forms with a twinkle in her eyes as both of them scanned her for injuries.

"I'm fine!" Star said. "I promise."

The moment her feet touched the ground, she found herself wrapped in Dakar's powerful arms. "Don't you ever do anything like that again," he said in a thick, husky tone before letting her go so Madas could wrap her arms around Star for a brief hug.

"I agree," Madas hissed gruffly. "My heart stopped when I saw you jump and again when you were hanging there."

Star hugged her friend back before she stepped back and surveyed the area. Her eyes widened in excitement when she saw the metal grill covering the narrow pipe used for directing rain water into the fortress.

The bars covering the entrance were about two feet apart. Star almost ran to the covering. She was getting closer and closer to Jazin. She could feel it. She glanced up at the sky. It was already beginning to get darker. She would need to move fast. She would cross the wire in the dark, relying on her skills and touch to guide her. It would be difficult, but she knew she could do it.

Once on the other side, she would follow through with the rest of their plans and shut down the control room at the top of the building. Madas and Dakar would then attach slide bars to the wire and slide down to the main tower without fear of triggering the defense system. Dakar could take care of the rest of the systems before helping her and Madas locate Jazin.

Madas reached around and pulled the bag containing the items Star would need from her back. "Remember, help will come from the man with glowing eyes. He is a friend. Do not fear him."

"I will," Star said as she knelt looking at the bars. "Look for my signal to know it is clear."

"We will," hissed Madas quietly. "Little warrior, believe in your skills and be safe."

Star nodded solemnly. "I'll be careful. I just want to get Jazin out of here and somewhere safe."

"Do you remember the configuration of the controls that work the above ground defense system?" Dakar asked.

Star nodded as she slid her feet through the bars. "Yes, I remember. Give me at least two hours," she said as she carefully lowered the rest of her body through the bars. It was a tight fit, even for her petite form. "Drop me the bag," she called up softly once she was through.

Madas dropped the small bag that she had been carrying inside her larger one. It contained the explosives Star would need, plus several weapons and a device that would override the controls for the doors. She stood back so Dakar could drop the last items she would need, her crossbow and arrows and a staff that extended out with a push of a button. Star would need that to help balance her as she crossed the wire.

"Two hours," Star called up to the two faces looking down at her before turning. "Show time," she muttered under her breath before she moved to the narrow piping that tunneled through the mountain.

* * *

"I'm going to chain my mate up when I get my claws on her," Gril Tal Mod growled out in fury as he studied the latest Intel that had come in.

They had wasted two days' worth of travel when they had followed one false trail. The one they now followed had been sent to them anonymously by an informant that told them information that only his mate could have told the male. Information she had shared with him and he had ignored.

Guilt and fear ate at him for not listening to her. This was something he would change the next time he got his mate under him. He would listen to her dreams and take them seriously in the future. If he had a chance in the future.

There will be a next time, he swore under his breath.

"Do we have any idea who the informant is?" Ajaska asked as he stared at Torak and Gril. "Torak, were you able to authenticate the video disk images that were sent?"

"They are authentic. I double checked them myself," Torak replied, looking at the three-dimensional image they had received that also included images of the prison fortress that was supposed to be holding his younger brother.

"There is no information on the informant, but he knew things only my mate could have told him," Gril said. "He knew things she would never have told anyone, even under torture," he added reluctantly.

"He also knew things about Jazin that only a few select people know about," Torak added.

Ajaska nodded as he studied the information they had and analyzed the best way to get his youngest son out alive. When Gril had come to him with the video disk and information that Jazin was alive and being held prisoner, Ajaska had been stunned. When River approached him and Torak that same morning with what Madas and Star had told her, he had been furious. Not with the delicate blue-eyed warrior, but with himself for having accepted that his youngest son had been killed without verifying the information personally.

He had let grief cloud his judgment. That was something he would never do again. Because of his lack of action, his son would have been lost without him ever knowing what had truly happened to him. He still might if they did not get to him soon enough.

His fists clenched under the table in fury at his former councilman. He should have killed Tai Tek when he first suspected he was behind the assassinations of some of the other members of the council. The fact that he didn't have concrete proof was the only thing that stopped him.

In the old days, he wouldn't have cared but the new Alliance set up guidelines for each star system. Killing members of your council just because you had a feeling they were murdering others was on the list of what was not allowed. The Alliance wanted proof first.

"The informant said he would contact us if they needed further assistance. I just hope we get there in time," Torak said. "The defense system at the fortress is a relatively new one set up by the Corazans. We can take it out, but it would alert Tai Tek and his guards they are under attack. There are several escape tunnels that lead out. We can also cover those. We have three A-Class warships and six C-Class. Each has over a hundred fighters on board."

"I have three Tearnat warships that will be arriving shortly. They each have fifty fighters on board and will cover the outer region for enemy starships," Gril added.

Ajaska nodded and leaned forward to study the layout of the prison. "What is this?" He asked, pointing to a darker area under the surface of the planet. The darker shape ran for a long distance not far from the fortress and appeared to be very deep.

"It is a natural ravine," Gril said. "It is over 200 meters deep. It weaves around three sides of the fortress. The backside is built into the mountain."

"Our best bet is to come in fast. Fighters can take out the laser cannons here, here, and here," Torak said pointing to the three largest cannons mounted up high. "We will drop attack transports here and here. They can come in and take heavy fire with little damage. Two fighters will come in from the east and south to take out the cannons along this wall. This will allow our ground troops to move in using additional armored transports."

"I will order additional troops to deploy from here," Gril said pointing to the mountain. "They can move down the side of the mountain easily."

"What of the west side?" Ajaska asked.

"That is where we suspect Jazin is being held. We will have to take it level by level. We cannot take a chance of firing on it and possibly killing him or burying him alive," Torak stated looking moodily at the image. "I only hope we can get to him before Tai Tek orders his execution. Truthfully, that is my biggest concern."

"He will already be out," a voice from the door said softly.

Torak turned and scowled at his mate. He had left her in their living quarters. He should have known better than to think she would stay there. He had planned to leave her on Kassis but one look at her face told him that was not likely to happen. His fingers moved to his temple that suddenly began to throb. It had a tendency to do that whenever his mate got that look in her eye.

"Why do you believe that, Lady River?" Gril asked, looking into the dark blue eyes of the unusual female.

"Because I know what I would do if I was in their place and Star would do the same," River replied calmly looking at the image floating above the table. "It isn't much different than on Trolis' warship," she murmured walking into the room and closer to the three-dimensional blueprint.

"Tell us how you would rescue my son," Ajaska asked quietly, looking intently at River's face as she studied the map.

"What is this?" River asked, pointing to a dark spot on the side of the mountain.

"It looks like a duct system for water. It is too small for the warriors to fit through and even if they could, they could not get down the mountain unseen or without triggering the defense system," Gril responded with a frown.

"A Tearnat or a Kassis warrior, perhaps, but not a petite circus performer," River said with a small lift of her lips. "What about this? What is it and where does it go?"

Torak frowned as he studied the thin cable. His eyes shifted to the tower where it connected. It would be impossible for a warrior to use it. If they tried to, they would be fired upon because the laser defense system reached up to within a few centimeters under it. The only way to cross it would be to.....

A curse burst from Torak and Ajaska's lips at the same time. "It would be suicide to try to cross that! It would have to be done after dark or she would be seen and there is no guarantee of the strength or integrity of the cable. It has probably been there since that fortress was constructed a hundred years or more ago," Torak said.

"And what would she do if she did make it?" Ajaska asked in disbelief. "She is only one small female. She would need to get into the control room and make her way down eight or more levels through a fortress full of seasoned warriors."

River smiled. "She'll figure out a way. Don't forget, she won't be alone. She has Madas, Dakar, Armet and our unknown informant to help her," River replied confidently. "We know how she'll get to the control tower. We just don't know how she is going to get Jazin out. We have to be ready for when she does. Because if there is one thing I know, it is this," River paused to look at each of the men sitting around the table before she continued. "If it were Torak, or Ajaska or any other member of my family, I would never stop, never give up until I had them back with me." She looked at Gril and smiled.

"Would you let anything stop you from getting to Madas?"

Gril thought of a time not that long ago. A time when he had been in a position similar to Jazin. Only then it was his mate who had been a prisoner and was sentenced to die. No, he would never give up, never let anything stop him. His large huge head swung around to look at the image again. This time he thought of what his mate would do. He thought like the warrior that she was. A smile curled back his thin lips, showing off his long, sharp teeth.

"I know how they plan to get Lord Jazin out," he growled out in a low, confident voice. "This is what we must do to help them."

Chapter 11

Star pushed the bag ahead of her. She could finally see the light at the end of the tunnel. It was faint but it was a light. She had moved through the pipe a little faster than she expected as it was bigger than they originally thought it would be.

She lifted her face to the steady breeze that was flowing through the aqueduct, trying to gauge the speed of it. The crossing was going to be difficult enough with the limited visibility. The last thing she needed was a big gust of wind trying to blow her off. She had done some outdoor aerial work, but not much. She hadn't told the others that though.

When she reached the end, she pulled herself into a sitting position and stared out at the huge fortress. Inside was the man she loved more than life itself. The slight breeze played with the strands of long, blond hair that had pulled loose from her braid and dried the sweat on her face, cooling her heated skin. Her eyes moved over the complex. High walls surrounded it on three sides where it blended into the mountain. It was beautiful in a medieval sort of way.

The walls were almost black and were slick, as if each block of stone had been fitted perfectly together and hand polished. Three high turrets adorned the walls with interconnecting walkways between them. Star could see the movement of warriors in the towers and on the walls.

Large and small mounted cannons lined the walls. Her eyes moved to the tall tower in the center. Just below the top, she could see an opening where a cannon was mounted. Her eyes roamed that building carefully, looking for potential threats. She counted two warriors in the tower.

She slid on a pair of the goggles Armet had given her. Adjusting the focus, she observed the men for several long minutes. They never looked up thankfully. She let her gaze move up to where the wire connected to the tall central tower.

It may have been placed as a ground wire so if the tower was struck by lightning it would travel through the wire into the mountain instead of damaging the tower. It was connected about five meters above the open center where the warriors stood. The roof curved, but there were hand and foot holds near where the wire was secured so maintenance could be done on it.

Star let her eyes focus in on the opening where the warriors were again. She would have to take them out. She couldn't trust to use the small, knock-out powder bombs that Madas made her. The area was too open and the breeze would be blowing it away from them. She would need to kill them; quickly and silently. The door she needed to access was inside where they were standing.

Her heart twisted at the idea of taking another life, but she would do whatever she had to do to rescue Jazin. It wasn't like she hadn't killed before, she reminded herself silently as she pulled the goggles from her head and stuffed them into the backpack.

She looked down from where she was sitting. She would have to climb down less than a meter to a narrow metal platform surrounding the cable she would be crossing. The diameter of the cable was actually a little thicker than what she was used to balancing on so she felt confident the crossing wouldn't be too difficult. Her eyes rose to the sky. She would start out in another ten minutes. In the meantime, she would organize her pack so she would have everything she needed handy.

"I'm coming for you Jazin," Star murmured softly into the twilight. "If you can feel me, I'm coming for you."

* * *

Jazin's head jerked up. He had fallen into a light sleep thanks in part to the utter exhaustion in his body and to the pain patches that still helped to relieve some of his discomfort. His eyes searched the darkness of his cell. He had heard Star's voice.

He could swear he could almost feel her warm breath against his skin. She was close. His eyes closed tightly as he fought against the fear that rose inside him like lava inside a volcano that could no longer contain it.

He had been left blissfully alone for the past few hours since Jarmen had left to see if he could pick up any signs of communication or get a feel for when Tai Tek was expected to return. A shudder rocked Jazin's body. He hoped the councilman hadn't returned. He was hanging onto life by a thread. He had only had the small amount of water and nutrients that Jarmen had brought him. Between the lack of food and water and blood loss from the torture his body had endured, he was extremely weak. Fear engulfed him at the thought of what would happen to Star if Tai Tek got his hands on her.

"Please, if you are listening," Jazin whispered quietly into the cold darkness surrounding him. "Please, keep her safe."

Before he had met Star, it had been years since he thought of the Gods that had liberated their world. Zephren, the God of War, his two sons and three daughters had come to their world thousands of years ago. The ancient scripts tell of a time when the people of Kassis had been almost extinct. Their world taken over by a cruel race of aliens who wanted to strip their world of everything that lived.

Zephren, his two sons and three daughters arrived on the night the twin moons of Kassis aligned with one another to form one moon. It was said to only happen once every two thousand years. The skies turned a dark purple from the fierce storm that raged in the heavens. Out of the storm, six great ships appeared in the skies over the last remaining cities of Kassis, each commanded by one of the Great Gods and the Goddesses.

The battle that followed was fierce, but by the end, the people of Kassis were free. His family was supposed to be descended from one of the Goddesses. The goddess was said to have fallen in love with the commander of the forces protecting the city where his home was located while her sisters were said to have fallen in love with his cousins.

It is said that is how the different clans had formed in an effort to make their world stronger. In fact, if he remembered the lessons he received when he was a boy, the garden located in the center of the Four Houses of Kassis is where his forefather and the Goddess were said to have sworn their love and the Royal Houses of Kassis were built for their children. He was named after that great warrior from long ago.

Now, he thought as he leaned his head back against the jagged wall, *I have my own alien warrior.*

How his ancestor dealt with having a mate who was in constant danger was beyond him. He could feel his gut twist at the thought of anything happening to Star. A small smile tugged at his lips as he thought of her mutinous glare after he had returned to his House with her.

She was constantly trying to sneak out or do things he felt were too much for her. Her blistering curses still stung his ears whenever he would catch her just as her heated kisses warmed his soul. A chuckle escaped as he remembered.

No, he thought, *I wouldn't want her any other way. I love her so much. I don't remember if I ever told her that. I have to live so I can tell her just how much she means to me.*

He pulled a pain patch he had hidden under a loose rock and slid it into place on his neck. If what Jarmen said was true, others knew where he was and would be coming for him. He would need to do what he could to help. He focused inward, trying to focus his mind and body on gathering the strength it would need when the time came.

Hope blossomed inside him as he realized he would not die alone in this unknown prison. A fierce burning rage began building with that hope. He would return home. He would not let his people down. He would not leave them vulnerable to attack. He was Jazin Ja Kel Coradon, the third son of the ruling House of Kassis, descendant of the Goddess and the great warrior Jazin. He would rise to protect his people as was his right as a Lord of Kassis.

He rose slowly, steadily as he felt the spirit of the warriors of old return to his mind and body. With concentrated effort, he began moving in a focused pattern. Slowly at first, before he increased the speed as his body responded to his commands. He ignored the torn flesh on his chest and back, he ignored the pull on the cuts or the ache from the bruises.

The pain patch was doing its job of blocking most of his discomfort. He turned, striking out in the age old dance of the warrior. He would be ready when his mate came. He would fight beside her as long as he could.

* * *

Star paused as she waited for the gust of wind to finish its twirling, shifting flow around her. It wasn't bad, but there were occasional gusts that threatened to unbalance her. She stood straight until it passed, the long staff in her hands tilting ever so slightly when she needed the additional balance on one side or the other. The shoes she had on were softer than the boots in the bag on her back. She kept the small crossbow and arrow tucked securely under the bag.

She stared straight ahead, feeling carefully with her toes as her eyes focused on the image at the end of the wire that she had in her head. She had descended from her hiding place just after dark and stepped onto the wire. She estimated she had just under a hundred meters to the tower.

She had paused four times as gusts gathered and danced around her, trying to unbalance her slight form. She refused to bend to it. Now, as the end approached, she focused on it. She was close enough to see where the wire was bolted into the heavy stone fortress. A search light danced under her briefly, but it was scanning far lower than where she stood.

She breathed out a silent sigh of relief as she stepped on the slanted roof of the tower. Leaning forward, she gripped one of the iron rings used as a foot and hand hold. She twisted and sat down, pulling the backpack and crossbow off her back. She tucked the backpack around one of the iron rings higher up before loading two arrows into the crossbow. She clenched another arrow between her teeth before she climbed down to the last ring.

Turning, she slid her feet under the ring and did a slow back bend. She would be hanging by her feet from the ring and firing the crossbow upside down. It would be similar to when she was doing some of her acts. She just needed to focus on the fact that the targets were a living, moving entity.

Arching her back, she slowly lowered her body using the muscles she had perfected over a lifetime of training. She barely reached past the edge of the roof. She remained still, her muscles straining as she carefully took aim. One warrior came around the corner to talk to the other man. She would have to be quick to kill them both.

"I need refreshments," the one warrior was saying to the other. "Do you want anything?"

"Bring me some food," the other grumbled as he moved the light in a slow arc. "I didn't get any dinner. Tai Tek's new Captain of the Guard ordered me up here instead. This is the third shift I have had without a break," he complained. "I am going to catch a few hours of sleep later."

"Might as well," the first warrior replied, stepping forward until he was in the way of the other man. "Nothing happens here. I don't mind, just don't let the Captain catch you," he muttered darkly. "He slit two of the warriors throats for complaining earlier."

"The first chance I get, I am off this rock," the man replied. "I can find better pay selling fighters to the fight rings on Elpidios than I do here."

"Maybe we can go in together," the man said before he turned to head towards the door. His eyes widened when he saw Star's long, blond braid hanging down below her.

Star fired the crossbow just as the man opened his mouth. He jerked back a step in surprise and looked down at the arrow protruding from his chest before collapsing to the floor. The first man turned in surprise and took a step forward, but that was as far as he got before Star released the second arrow, hitting him in the throat.

The man's strangled gasp was soft, but seemed to echo loudly in Star's sensitive ears. She quickly pulled herself back up. Twisting, she grabbed the backpack and slid it over her shoulders.

She left the staff balanced on the rings and clipped the crossbow securely to her side before climbing back down to the last ring. She turned facing the top of the roof and did a handstand, holding onto the ring before letting her body fall over the side of the roof and swinging into the open area. She tucked and rolled, coming up on one knee and quickly threaded another arrow into the crossbow. After making sure she was alone except for the two dead bodies, she tapped the small device hooked to her ear to turn it on.

"I'm in," she whispered before she turned the device back off.

Star removed the backpack and pulled out the three items she would need to take down the defense system. She pulled the woven mask over her face, making sure it was secure before she pulled out two of the small round, clay powder balls that Madas had made for her. The last thing she pulled out was the device to unlock the door without alerting those inside.

She stood up and walked over to the narrow doorway. A panel was lit next to it. Star attached the device and pressed the button Dakar showed her. She waited impatiently, looking around her as a series of lights on the panel changed from red to green.

Her eyes skirted the two men she had killed. She refused to feel remorse. Those men had made their choice when they decided to work for Tai Tek. From what she heard before she shot them, they planned on doing other things that would have hurt others as well.

The last light turned and the door in front of her opened silently. Star stepped in and turned, facing the door as it closed behind her. There would be no turning back now.

* * *

"She's in," Dakar called out quietly to Madas who was working her way down the side of the mountain.

"We are almost to the cable," Madas responded in a soft hiss.

Dakar glanced down. He could see the cable as clear as day with the night goggles on. Madas had not needed any. He was learning some very interesting things about his Tearnat companion. She had a spunk about her that the women of Kassis lacked. She also had a strange sense of humor that he liked.

She had offered to carry him on her back down the side of the mountain if he wanted. When he had bit back an angry retort she had dissolved in giggles that told him she knew he would have never accepted such help. When he threatened to tell Gril about her offer she had blushed furiously.

"I wouldn't if I were you," she hissed out as she ducked her head.

"Why? Do you think he would be upset to know that you had another male wrapped around you?" Dakar had asked with a raised brow enjoying watching the female Tearnat shift uncomfortably.

Madas long lashes rose and she looked at Dakar with a small smile. "He can be very jealous. If you were on my back, he might think you were trying to mount me," she hissed out with a chuckle. "Not that you would, but he would not see it as that."

Dakar's eyes widened as he studied Madas. She was very beautiful in her own way. Her long lashes framed midnight colored eyes that glittered often with humor, compassion, and intelligence. He let his eyes run down over the slender curve of her head and neck before traveling down her body. She was different, but she beautiful.

"I wouldn't be so sure, Lady Madas," Dakar said with a slight curve to his lips in return. "You are a very beautiful lady. It is hard to ignore that and I am sure your mate is more aware of your beauty than you appear to be," he responded before disappearing over the edge of the mountain.

Madas' eyes widened as Dakar's words sank in and she blushed an even darker green as his eyes roamed over her. Never before had she thought that another male would look at her with desire the way Gril did. The fact that the Kassisan warrior saw her as a desirable female stunned her. She would have to ask her mate about it. Madas pictured Gril's face when she related what the warrior had just said and decided maybe, just maybe, it would be better not to say anything after all.

Madas jumped down, landing lightly on the metal access ledge surrounding the cable. A moment later, Dakar landed beside her. He quickly scanned the open area where Star had said she was at. He did not see anything which meant she had already accessed the lift that would take her down to the control room. He drew in a deep, calming breath, trying to calm the nerves that twisted inside him at the thought of what would happen to Star if she was caught.

He turned when he felt a slender hand brush his arm. "She will be fine," Madas said, looking not at Dakar, but at the tower across from them.

"Defenses down," a soft voice suddenly caressed his ear.

"She has taken the control room," Dakar said harshly as the breath he drew in earlier was released in relief. "Let's go."

Madas attached the hand bar to the wire and launched herself over the edge. The slight downward angle allowed her to slide at a steady rate of decline. She swung into the opened area the moment she was close enough and turned. Her arm reached out and grabbed Dakar around the waist as he came in after her a little faster than he thought. She steadied him before quickly releasing him and stepping back.

"Thanks," Dakar said gruffly.

"Let us get Lord Jazin and get out of here," Madas said, nodding toward the two dead men. "I expect

there will be many more before we are through. I
would just as soon not be one of them."

Dakar nodded and stepped toward the lift. The
device was still attached to it so they could enter. He
pressed the device and the lift opened. Pulling the
device off the key panel, he stepped inside the lift and
waited for Madas before pressing the inside panel.
Within moments they were descending rapidly down
the tower to the ground floor control room. Both he
and Madas pulled their laser pistols out in
preparation. They wanted no surprises.

* * *

Star turned as the door opened to the control
room, drawing the crossbow around in front of her.
She was about to release the arrow she had ready
when the glowing eyes froze her finger on the trigger.
She stared at the face intently before a frown twisted
her face into a scowl.

"Well, are you going to come in or are you going
to let everyone and their brother know that
something is going on?" She asked impatiently.

She turned back to the control panel and focused
on what she had been doing. Armet told her to
disable the communications system so that the
warriors could not send and receive instructions. She
was trying to find the panel he showed her in the
diagram.

"What are you trying to do?" The raspy, deep
voice asked hesitantly.

Star glanced over her shoulder at the hooded
figure. "Armet and Dakar said I needed to disable

their communications systems, but I can't find the panel that looks like the one they showed me," she complained.

"I will disable it," the man replied quietly.

Star watched as his amber eyes appeared to swirl with color as he focused for a moment. "It is disabled," he replied before turning his head.

Jarmen went to take a step back, but stopped in surprise as a tiny, slender hand touched his arm. He jerked in surprise at the feel of another being touching him, even if it was through the material of his shirt. His eyes fastened on the light blue ones staring at him intently.

"Is he still alive?" The husky voice of the female asked with a tremble in it. "Jazin. Is my mate alive?"

"Yes," Jarmen responded. "His lives."

Star's eyes filled with tears and she sniffed before she moved close enough so she could wrap her arms tightly around Jarmen's waist. "Thank you. Thank you so much for everything. I'll never be able to repay you for what you have done," she choked out.

Jarmen stared over the head of the female who had her arms wrapped tightly around him. Warmth flooded his system as feelings he had never encountered before tore through him. This is what it meant to receive a hug.

His brain processed the information it was receiving and analyzed the effects on his body. He breathed in deeply. Shock flowed through him at the resulting reaction. He was able to detect every scent and break it down to its most elemental form. The classification of flowers that mixed with her hair follicle, the lotion she had with another delicate scent, the salt, sweat, and natural aroma of her skin. All of it came to him and was processed, analyzed and stored.

His arms closed lightly around her wanting to see if the feel of her skin matched what he had read about. The sensors on the tips of his fingers picked up the texture and he almost groaned at the softness. His own skin covering was not as soft as this and the times he had touched Jazin to help him stand or to grasp his hand had never felt this soft, delicate, and smooth.

The door leading from the tower opened suddenly. Jarmen immediately went into defense mode, turning so his body was between the door and the female in his arms. He raised his arm, several beams of light focused on the center of Madas and Dakar's chests as his head turned toward them. The male thrust the female Tearnat he met on the outer edges behind him and raised his own weapon.

"You the informant?" Dakar asked harshly.

"You the rescue party?" Jarmen asked briefly in return.

Dakar kept his weapon aimed at Jarmen, but raised his other hand, palm out in greeting. "Yes. Now, let go of Lady Star or I'll blow your head off," he gritted out.

Madas chuckled behind him, pulling Dakar's attention away for a brief moment. It was long enough for Jarmen to assess the protective tone the male had for both females. Jarmen reluctantly released the tiny female in his arms and stepped back. He was surprised that this was the first time he really looked around the room. He had been so fascinated by the tiny female he had not even assessed the room. He quickly counted ten unconscious forms. Frowning, he looked at the female again trying to understand how she could have taken out so many warriors at one time.

"What is this?" Jarmen asked, gently touching the woven mask covering the lower half of Star's face.

"A plant fiber mask that Madas made for me. It protects me from the knock-out bombs she gave me," she replied pulling the mask down.

Jarmen breathed in deeply. He could faintly pick up the residue from the plant pollen in the air. He shook his head as a slight wave of dizziness threatened him. He would need to analyze it more in-depth when he returned to his home. For now, they needed to hurry. It was late so many of the guards were sleeping, but that would not last long once someone tried to use the communications system and realized it no longer worked.

"We must hurry before they become aware that something is wrong," Jarmen said. "I will take you to Jazin. Dakar and I will carry him out. Are you capable of defending us should the need arise?" He asked, looking first at Star then at Madas.

Both women looked at him with a raised eyebrow. He wasn't sure what that meant, but hoped it was a yes. He was about to turn away when he froze. An incoming message was being transmitted. Tai Tek had returned and he wasn't alone.

Jarmen turned his head and looked at the three warriors standing near him. "It is too late. Tai Tek has returned. I will detain him and his men as long as possible while you rescue Jazin. Go to the end of this corridor, down two levels, turn left for the next two turns then three rights and down another level. He is in the fifth cell. I will return if I can. Hurry, Tai Tek has brought additional warriors with him."

Star watched wide-eyed as the man with the glowing amber eyes disappeared through the door and down the opposite way he told them to go. She started when Madas gripped her arm and started pulling her out the door and down toward the stairs at the end of the corridor. Her heart began beating as adrenaline kicked in. Dakar followed closely behind them.

"How will we carry Jazin if he can't walk?" Star asked as they hurried down the stairs.

"I have something that will help," Dakar muttered behind her. "Don't worry, we will get him out of here."

Chapter 12

Ajaska stared at the information coming in. There were almost a dozen Elpidios warships in orbit around the small planet. With the nine Kassisan warships and the three Tearnat warships that were just coming into orbit they were evenly matched in number. The biggest difference was the technology.

The Kassisan warships were superior while the Tearnat and Elpidios were evenly matched in not only technology, but in their viciousness in fighting. Ajaska had only had the privilege of meeting a Elpidios warrior once before. Actually, it was three Elpidios warriors and he was lucky to have survived the incident.

He rubbed the back of his neck and glanced at his oldest son in discomfort. He had never mentioned the encounter simply because he could barely remember most of it. He had been very drunk at the time and had been much younger. All he could really remember was he barely made it out with his life and a massive hangover the next morning.

"Sir, we are being hailed," the ensign at the communications console called out breaking into his thoughts.

"Open communications," Ajaska said, standing up straight and clasped his hands behind his back with a silent prayer to the Gods.

The Gods were obviously not listening at the moment, he thought in resignation when he recognized the face in the center of the view screen.

He winced as the face that appeared in front of him turned dark as surprise and something else flashed across it. He wasn't the only one who remembered a little more about that night so many years ago. A sigh was wrenched from deep down as he studied the face he had hoped to never see again. It was a little older like him, but he would never forget it.

"Greetings *âme soeur,*" the voice said coldly. "Much time has passed since you disappeared."

"Mena," Ajaska responded coolly.

"So, you remember me?" The tall female said with a sarcastic chuckle. "Why are you here?"

"My son has been taken prisoner," Ajaska responded harshly. "I have no quarrels with the Elpidios, but I do with Tai Tek and those responsible for his abduction."

The light blue skinned female rose slowly from the center chair. Torak looked at his father with a raised eyebrow of inquiry before he turned back to the commander of the Elpidios warship. He stepped closer to his father, standing just to his right and behind him in silent support.

"Another of your sons?" Commander Mena Rue stated looking at Torak with clear, intelligent eyes. "Did your father tell you he was mated to not one, but three Elpidios warriors at one time before he disappeared?"

The tightening around Torak's mouth was the only indication that he did not know. Commander Mena Rue's lips twisted into a smirk before she looked Ajaska up and down. She felt a shiver run through her as she thought back to the few hours of pleasure she had enjoyed with the huge Kassis warrior almost forty years before. She wondered at the time if it had been her imagination or the excessive drink that made the memory more than it really was, but as she stared at the broad chest, she had to secretly admit it was neither.

"What proof do you have that the Kassisan councilman has your son?" Commander Mena Rue asked sharply.

"My son is there," Ajaska bit out in response without answering her question.

Mena didn't point out that obvious fact. She had a squadron of warships to think about instead of a misplaced soul mate who had been nothing more than a one night stand many years ago.

Her commanding officer had ordered her to secure the needed crystals that the Kassisan had promised. Their world was dying and needed the energy the crystals could give to work the necessary shields to protect it from the radiation that was slowly killing it. They had a way of preventing the death of the planet. What they did not have was the energy source to do it. She had been told to not return unless she had at least one supply ship filled with the life-giving energy crystals.

Tai Tek had approached the leader of her world with a promise. In return for their help in ridding the corrupted ruling family of Kassis, he would give them access to all the crystals they would ever need. She had been skeptical about the man's promise. Hell, she didn't even like him and neither did the Supreme Admiral, but the Grand Ruler had ordered the mission.

Now, she was faced with a deadly armed force that outmatched hers. If she refused, she could probably take out a few of the ships, but there was no doubt in her mind that she would lose all of hers. She studied the huge male and his son and knew that they would fight to the death to retrieve their missing family member.

Her eyes shifted to another figure that came up from behind the two men standing in front of the viewport. Her eyes widened in surprise as a petite female with the dark blue eyes of their oceans moved to stand near the younger version of Ajaska. Something about the female tugged at a distant memory. Mena's frown turned even darker as the knowledge stayed just out of her reach.

"Since when do the Kassis allow females aboard their warships?" Mena asked with a raised eyebrow.

"That is not what is important right now," Ajaska said, straightening to his full height as worry for Jazin's safety pressed down on him. "Is Tai Tek on board one of your ships?"

Mena looked at the dark fury burning in the eyes of the Kassis leader and decided right then and there she would not oppose him. Getting herself and those under her killed would not get them the desperately needed power crystals. Besides, something was telling her that the Elpidios Grand Ruler was talking to the wrong Kassisan if he wanted them. She relaxed her stance to show less aggression in the hopes that they would be able to get out of this alive.

"No, he was aboard his own ship and has already returned to the surface," Mena said. "The Elpidios have no quarrel with you, Lord Ajaska. We were merely concluding a transaction for crystals that our world desperately needs. If you need assistance in securing your son, I offer myself and my ships in support."

"I appreciate the offer but do not think it will be necessary," Ajaska responded coolly. "Let your Grand Ruler know that if he wants to negotiate for crystals to contact my son, Torak, or myself," Ajaska added harshly. "Tai Tek is a traitor to our world. He will be executed for his part in trying to assassinate the royal family. The same goes for any other who think to harm the Royal House of Kassis."

Mena bowed her head in understanding of the unspoken message; get out or die. Her eyes turned to the female who was standing silently next to Lord Torak. Her eyes widened in disbelief as the memory that floated on the edges of her mind suddenly solidified.

With a silent curse, she motioned for the communications officer to cut the open link. The moment it was done, Commander Mena Rue turned and barked out commands to those commanding the other ships. They needed to return to Elpidios as soon as possible. If what she remembered was true, life was about to get very, very interesting.

Mena walked into the commander's room off the bridge and sat down at the console built into the desk. The unique beep reserved for communications between fleet commanders sounded. She grimaced when she saw who was identified on the link. She debated on what she should tell the Grand Ruler before deciding on the truth. Perhaps the new information she had would be even more useful than the promise of a Kassisan traitor.

* * *

Dakar raised his hand silently to stop Star and Madas. He listened carefully, then motioned that guards were approaching. Star raised the crossbow, pressing it snugly against her shoulder as she moved back against the wall. Out of the corner of her eye, she could see Dakar's fist tighten around the laser pistol he held in one hand. Madas' quiet breath sounded close to her ear as her friend pressed against her back.

They had already dispatched five guards on their way down from the control room. They were on the second level and had one more to go. Dakar took a deep breath and spun out into the corridor firing as he went. Star turned in the opposite direction covering his back. She fired one arrow into a guard as he raised his arm to fire at Dakar. The blast from his laser hit the wall right above her head instead as he collapsed face first into the cold stone floor.

"Clear," Star said in a calm voice the belied how she was really feeling.

"Let's go," Dakar grunted out. "We have one more level, then we need to get out of here as soon as possible."

Madas motioned for Star to go ahead of her as she followed Dakar down another long corridor before coming upon another set of narrow, winding steps. They rapidly moved down them. Dakar paused as he approached the last few steps.

"Let me check it out first," he whispered.

"No, we don't have time," Star hissed. "You heard the informant. Tai Tek is here. I won't give him a chance to get to Jazin before we do!"

Dakar's mouth tightened, but that was the only thing that showed his disagreement. He nodded instead and moved down the last steps that opened into a long, dark narrow corridor. He glanced around the corner but didn't see anyone. He stepped into the opening and began counting the doors, pausing at the fifth one.

"Lord Jazin," Dakar called out quietly, looking into the small square cut in the door to see if he could see anything.

"Dakar?" Jazin responded hoarsely.

"Yes, my lord," Dakar said in relief. "Give me a second to get the door open."

* * *

Jazin swayed dizzily for a moment before he locked his muscles. Sweat stung the numerous cuts as it ran down his body, but he ignored it. At least he was still standing, he thought in relief.

When he heard the footsteps approaching, he had feared it was either the guards or Tai Tek returning. He was prepared to fight. He would not be tortured again. He relaxed his fingers, dropping the rock that was cutting into his palm. His mouth went dry to the point he couldn't even ask Dakar about Star.

The door opened suddenly and a small, delicate shape burst through it answering his unspoken question. Star's soft cry of rage filled the cold, dark cell as she rushed toward Jazin's swaying form.

"Jazin," she cried out, dropping the crossbow on the floor so she could wrap her arms around him.

Jazin's body collapsed in on itself at her tender touch. He was vaguely aware of Star and Madas' arms controlling his descent to the floor. A part of him wanted to rage at his weakness. He did not want his mate to see him too weak to protect her. It was his place to be strong. Unfortunately, his body wasn't in the mood to agree with what his mind was trying to tell it.

"What have they done to you?" Star whispered, running her hand over his bruised and battered face. "Madas, you have to help him."

Madas looked up at Dakar with concern. "He is very weak. We must get him to the starship as soon as possible."

"I've notified Armet we are in and warned him Tai Tek had returned," Dakar said coming to kneel next to Jazin. "He will be in the center courtyard in twenty minutes. Jazin, I need to give you a Fast Patch," Dakar said grimly.

"What is a Fast Patch?" Star asked when she heard the hesitancy in Dakar's voice as he spoke to Jazin.

Dakar reached into the bag he was carrying and pulled out a container of water and a small package. He ripped the package open, revealing a small round yellow patch. He held the water to Jazin's mouth, letting a small amount flow into it before repeating the procedure until about a quarter of the container was gone. Once he felt Jazin had enough water to handle the dose of medicine his system he was about to receive, he moved to place the patch in the center of Jazin's chest over his heart.

Star's hand shot out stopping him before he could place it. "What is a Fast Patch?" She asked again, this time there was a trace of steel in her voice.

Dakar glanced at Star before he looked down at Jazin's still face. "It will accelerate the healing process. Within minutes of being absorbed into the system, his body will begin healing itself," Dakar stated grimly.

"What are you not telling me?" Star asked, tightening her grip on his wrist.

"What he is not telling you is there is a side effect," Madas said quietly. "The medicine will cause him to become very, very aggressive. It will give him added strength and will inhibit pain. I have seen it used only once before because of its side effects. It took many men to restrain the man given the dosage and he had to be contained in a cage for many hours until the medicine was completely out of his system. This is why it is banned."

Star looked at Jazin's labored breathing. Her hand trembled as she touched his cold, clammy skin. She let her gaze moved down over the torn flesh of his shoulders, chest, and stomach. A large discoloration around his ribs stood out, telling her he probably had several broken ribs.

"Will it kill him?" She asked quietly, refusing to look at the two people waiting for her decision.

"No," Dakar said with quiet confidence. "But, I can't promise he won't try to kill us."

Star's head jerked up and she glared at Dakar. "He would never hurt me. I'll keep him under control. You just get us the fuck out of here as fast as you can," she said as she released Dakar's wrist.

Dakar nodded before slapping his hand down on Jazin's chest. He stood up and moved back toward the door. Madas laid her hand on Star's shoulder and gave it a light squeeze before she stood and moved toward the door as well. They both turned and looked warily at Jazin.

Almost immediately, Star could see a change in Jazin's breathing and color. His skin grew warm, then almost hot to the touch. His breathing became steadier, faster. Her eyes widened as smaller cuts and bruises began to disappear right before her eyes. One minute she was kneeling next to Jazin's still body, the next moment she was lying on her back under it.

A deep, animalistic snarl echoed around the cell. Madas let out a cry of protest and stepped forward only to be stopped when Dakar wrapped an arm around her waist. Jazin's eyes flashed at Madas as he pressed his body down over Star's smaller one, pinning her to the floor under him.

"Don't," Dakar murmured urgently in Madas' ear. "He is marking her as his. If you try to stop him, he will attack and kill us both. He does not recognize any of us, but he recognizes her scent. He will do anything to protect her."

Jazin's low growled reverberated as his eyes swung to Dakar. "Mine!" He snarled, wrapping his arm around Star's tiny waist and pulling her up against his body. "Mine!" He repeated, turning to look at Star's wide, frightened eyes with a fierce possessive look.

"Star," Madas whispered. "We need to leave. I hear footsteps approaching."

Star turned her head even as Jazin stood with her still trapped against him. Her body hanging against his like a rag doll. She nervously licked her dry lips. She needed to get through to him that they were not the ones he needed to fight.

"Jazin," Star said, slowly raising her arm up so she could lay her palm against his hot cheek. "Sweetheart, we need to leave. The bad guys are coming and they want to hurt you again. I won't let them ever hurt you again, but I can't fight all of them. We need to follow Dakar and Madas. They are our friends. Can you do that?" Star asked in a trembling voice.

Jazin turned his head and sniffed Star's wrist before he opened his mouth and ran his tongue over the rapidly beating pulse. "Mine," he purred.

"Yes, I'm yours but the bad men will hurt me, kill me, if they catch me," Star whispered desperately as she saw Dakar and Madas motioning for her to hurry. "Please, help me. I'm scared."

Jazin's eyes narrowed and he growled again. "Go!" He snarled, turning with Star in his arms still.

"Put me down," Star begged. "We can move faster if I follow you."

Jazin shook his head forcibly, but Star pushed against him, pleading softly, until he reluctantly let her slide down his long length. Even as her feet touched the ground, his fingers locked around her wrist like an iron shackle. She barely had time to scoop up her crossbow before she was pulled through the door and into the dark corridor.

"This way," Dakar muttered. "There is a hidden set of steps. If we are lucky, Tai Tek won't be aware of them."

Chapter 13

Star's side hurt, but she refused to complain or slow down. Not that she had much choice in the matter. Jazin was being a wild man at the moment. The narrow, hidden passage at the opposite end of the corridor had been a surprise. It reminded Star of some of the hidden passages in the English castles her, Jo, and River toured one summer between shows. The architecture was very similar making her wonder if perhaps humans were really the descendants of aliens after all.

She stumbled as they neared the top. Jazin immediately whipped around and wrapped his other arm around her, pressing her against the wall. He buried his nose in her neck and licked a drop of sweat as it trailed down along the side of her silky skin. He pressed closer, grinding his pelvis into hers. She choked back the squeak of surprise that threatened to alert everyone in the fortress to their location when she felt his hard erection.

"You have got to be joking me!" She hissed out, wiggling in an effort to get free. "You are horny? Now?"

Madas soft chuckle barely reached her ears, but it was enough to let her know that her friend heard her startled exclamation. Star's face burned with embarrassment. Jazin continued to rub against her, licking and sucking on her neck, shoulder and earlobe like they were a couple of horny teenagers in the back of a matinee.

"Will you stop that!" Star hissed in his ear as his hand reached up under her shirt searching for her breast.

Dakar rolled his eyes before he motioned for Madas to go ahead of him. "I told you the medicine makes him more aggressive."

"Aggressive I can understand. But horny?" Star muttered as she fought to grab the hand that had found her small breast and was pulling at her nipple. She moaned as she felt her body respond. "Jazin not now, damn it!"

"Someone comes!" Madas hissed out pressing back against the dark opening.

Ten guards came rushing down the corridor. A silent curse burst from Dakar's lips before he let out a roar of rage and pulled his laser sword. In such close confines, the laser pistol would be too dangerous. The blasts would ricochet off the smooth, polished walls like sunlight on a mirror.

He cut three down almost immediately before the others regrouped and fought back. Madas charged into the melee, swirling and slicing with her sharp claws and slamming attackers back with her tail. Three of the guards circled around, spying Jazin. Star's eyes blazed with pure hatred when she saw one with a long, lighted whip he was unfurling.

"Oh, like hell no!" She snapped out, raising the crossbow over Jazin's shoulder and releasing an arrow.

The guard dropped the laser whip and grabbed his chest. He looked at Star's blazing eyes in disbelief before he fell backwards, dead. Star wasn't finished. She released two additional arrows. One pierced the throat of the other guard while the other hit the third guard in the shoulder, knocking him backwards into Madas who turned and swiped her unsheathed claws across his neck.

Jazin released Star, thrusting her behind him as two more guards came at him. He snarled, charging at them. He rolled at the last minute, snatching up the laser whip and flowed back to his feet behind them.

With a flick of his wrist, he wrapped one end of the whip around one of the guard's neck and pulled it back with an adrenaline filled jerk. The man's body continued forward even as his severed head fell backwards. Star's scream echoed in the corridor as she watched in horror. The second guard rushed for Star, determined to use her as a shield. He never made it. Jazin jumped, landing on his back and twisting his neck with a savage jerk.

He looked up into Star's horrified eyes and snarled. "Mine! Mine to protect."

He stood up and walked toward where she was pressed against the wall. He stopped in front of her and gazed down into her light blue eyes for what seemed an eternity. For a moment, doubt and reason fought for control of his drug-crazed mind.

"Star," Jazin muttered in a small, confused voice.

Star could see Jazin fighting for sanity. For just a brief second, she saw his eyes clear and concern and love shine through the medicine coursing through his system. She lifted her hand and gently touched his cheek, a small smile of understanding curved her lips.

"You are safe now," she whispered right before the glaze clouded his eyes again.

Jazin reached out and gripped Star by the waist, raising her up until her face was even with his. He crushed his lips against hers in a dark, possessive kiss that burned with barely suppressed desire and violence. Dakar's voice broke through the heated promise of possession.

"Move," Dakar yelled out wiping blood from his face as the last man fell to the floor. "Jarmen says Tai Tek has two dozen or more men headed this way."

Jazin's head jerked up at the sound of the familiar names. He fought to bring an image into his clouded mind to match the first name, but all he could picture where burning amber eyes. He turned, rolling his shoulder and wrapped his large hand around the small wrist.

The female's name had whispered through his mind, but he couldn't remember it now. All he knew was her scent called to him to mate, possess, claim, and kill any who would try to take her from him. Everything in him narrowed down to getting her away from everyone. He had to get her alone, somewhere safe, and when he did, he would lay his claim to her.

"He has killed all but Tai Tek and the men he just brought," Dakar murmured as he pressed his hand to his ear where his comlink was located. "He says they are headed this way and there are at least fifty of them total."

"Go," Jazin said with a jerk of his head.

Dakar nodded and stepped over the bodies of the dead guards. Jazin lifted Star into his arms, holding her face against his shoulder as he followed. Some part deep inside him knew that this was not something his mate was used to. Her horror had cut through him as she stared at him. It hurt worse than the injuries to his body.

Even as he thought that, he knew his body was healing at a rapid rate. He could actually feel the skin pulling and knitting together. He felt the bones in his ribs shifting and the calcium in his bones bridging the gaps between the broken pieces. He could even feel the blood replicating and replenishing his diminished supply.

His mind was a whirlwind of blinding rage and desperate need. Every breath the female took, every sound from her lips, every touch of her skin drove him out of his mind with the need to take her. Her scent alone was enough to make him want to drop to the floor or press her up against a wall and impale her on his throbbing shaft.

It was only the part of him that recognized she was in danger that prevented him from doing what his body and mind were demanding. The predator's need to protect his mate from danger overrode everything else.

They were almost to the ground level when two dozen well-armed men came at them from what seemed like every direction possible. The resounding roar of the men as they rushed forward was deafening. Dakar and Jazin both responded by pushing the two women in between them.

Star quickly loaded the crossbow, firing arrow after arrow into the group of attackers until she had exhausted her limited supply. She pulled the knives River had given her and began throwing them with the deadly accuracy she had learned from River and her parents. When she was down to her last knife, she held it.... waiting. Dakar and Madas were working to keep the guards coming from their front and left from getting any closer while Jazin was moving with lightning speed, cutting a path through the guards coming up from behind them.

Star twirled around when she heard Madas cry out in pain. She watched as her friend fell backwards over the body of a dead guard, blood pouring from a wound in her leg. One of the guards let out a roar and raised his laser sword, preparing to embed it through Madas' chest. Star screamed as she threw the knife she held tightly in her fist. The blade struck with such force it knocked the man back several steps before he collapsed.

Star raced toward where Madas lay on the floor. She scooped up one of the laser swords beside the dead body of another guard and charged forward. Jazin and Dakar were too busy to see what had happened.

Star twirled, slicing through the stomach of one attacker before bending almost backwards as another flicked a laser whip through the air. She saw the lighted tail as if it was in slow motion as it arched within centimeters of her chest. She straightened as the tail withdrew.

Madas thrust upward with the sword she had clutched in her bloody fist from where she lay on the floor. The man's screams of pain filled the chamber along with the other sounds. Star stumbled as she made her way over to Madas as two more guards rushed them.

Her arms trembled with fatigue, but she would never let anyone hurt her friend as long as she was standing. She thrust forward at the same time as one of the guards kicked out, catching her in the stomach with such force that it lifted her off the floor and flung her back several feet where she landed hard on the cold, stone floor.

Star struggled to draw in a breath of air. Everything was fuzzy on the edges. She clutched at her stomach, but was unable to catch her breath. Darkness blurred her vision, even as she heard Jazin's roar of rage, Madas' horrified cry, and Dakar's shout of denial.

I'm so sorry, Star thought, *I love you so much.*

Time slowed down until she could swear she could see the smallest dust mote as it drifted through the air. She saw Jazin twirling in rage at the men who had rushed her. The man who had kicked her fell to his knees under the force of the blows from Jazin's sword. His head fell away from his body as he toppled over.

Madas rose up, balancing on one leg and her tail swinging the double-sided battle ax. Dakar killed one guard before another thrust his sword into his side. She heard his cry before he turned and struck the man down.

Out of a dark passage, a man appeared. He was tall, muscular and had the most beautiful glowing eyes, she had ever seen. He moved through the few guards that remained striking with a deadly precision.

As the last man fell, all three turned to look at where Star lay unmoving. Her eyes slowly closed as Jazin's lithe form moved through the maze of dead bodies.

She tried to open her eyes, but it was too difficult. "You are safe now," Jazin whispered as he gently lifted her small body up.

Star gave in to the darkness as it surrounded her. Her arms falling limply as she was lifted with impossible care. The burning light calling her home.

* * *

"Where am I?" Star asked as she looked around her in wonder and confusion.

The world where she was standing looked like it came out of a Van Gogh painting. Small thatched roofs were barely visible in the distance. The sky was a deep purple. A stark contrast to the fields of gold. A few trees dotted the landscape of rolling hills leading to the edge of distant mountains. Huge birds soared high in the sky, their large red, yellow, and green feathers standing out. White clouds dotted the sky like a child's first finger painting.

Star turned in a circle in the golden grass. It was almost as tall as her. The sounds of birds taking flight had her shading her eyes to see what had startled them. Her eyes widened as huge space ships broke through the atmosphere.

She watched in horror as the ships fired on the thatched roofs of the village. She couldn't see anything due to the smoke that filled the bright, beautiful sky, but she could hear the screams.

She turned as the painting she was in seemed to melt around her, the colors twisting, blurring, blending together until a night sky filled with millions of brilliant points of light were the only light to see by. The night sky was not black but a rich, dark blue.

It reminded Star of River's eyes. Swirls of a lighter blue danced through the painted night, flowing like a river through the universe. She could almost swear she could see movement in the heavenly stream.

Star's breath caught as the stars began to fall around her like a light rain. They seemed so real she actually lifted her hands up to cup them as they fell around her. The sky lightened as more and more stars fell until she was surrounded by the glowing embers. She reached down and picked up one glowing ember and gazed into it.

Inside, she could see a battle. A man that looked like Jazin was leading a group of warriors against an alien race unlike anything she had ever seen. The twisted bodies were huge and resembled the praying mantas back home. The light flickered and died. The skies around her turned to red and she shivered. The color of blood surrounded her.

Jazin was standing on a hill that was now blackened and dry. His face reflected such a deep grief it tore at her. But, there was also a determination to survive, to fight on that she could only admire. Star turned to see what he was looking at.

In the distance, small fighters were coming out of the sky like the stars she had just imagined. They attacked the alien species advancing on Jazin and his warriors. The fight was fierce, but it was short as Jazin and his warriors rode into the fury of battle with a loud war cry.

The red dissolved until the ground glowed with the lighted crystals. All around her were the glittering stones. New life grew around her as the crystals absorbed into the ground, growing and spreading. She turned as Jazin walked out from a lone tree that still stood tall and proud on the side of the hill. A fierce storm raged in the dark purple skies, lightning arced as if in a grand display of fireworks.

One of the fighters that had fought the alien creatures landed a short distance away. Jazin didn't move. He was a huge, bear of a man. Muscles tensed and flexed as he kept one hand firmly on the sword clutched in it. His eyes were a piercing black. Star turned toward the fighter again, fascinated.

The dark, hooded top slid back and a figure rose out from it. The body was small, almost childlike in size. Star couldn't see what the creature looked like because of the helmet and uniform, but she could tell it was humanoid in appearance. Her eyes followed the figure as it advanced to within just a few steps of Jazin.

"Who are you?" Jazin demanded in a low fierce tone.

The figure reached up and slowly removed the helmet covering its head. With a shake, long flowing locks of white blond hair fell in waves down the woman's back. Star gasped as she gazed at an image that could have been an exact replica of her silhouetted against the stormy, dark purple sky.

The female smiled before speaking in a strangely accented voice. "Starla," came the softly spoken response. She raised her hand out in greeting. "From a distant planet known as Earth."

Jazin studied the outstretched hand silently before he grasped it in his larger one and tugged the small female forward into his arms. "I am Jazin. I claim you as mine," he responded with a slight curve of his lips before he crushed her lips with his own.

* * *

Star moaned as hot waves of need flowed through her body. She was burning. The scene of Jazin and her so long ago blended with the hot feel of hands on her own body. She felt like those stars that had fallen around her.

Her body arched in pleasure as a hot tongue swiped over her swollen nipples. Colors swirled into focus as her eyes opened in a dazed haze of desire. A cry ripped from her as the hands on her moved down her body, touching, stroking, igniting flames as they went.

"Jazin," Star cried out.

"Mine," a deep voice growled near her ear. "All mine."

Star jerked as she felt a long, hard shaft of silky skin pressed against her swollen vaginal channel. Hard hands gripped her, lifting her hips up off the soft narrow bed under her. With one thrust, Jazin impaled his throbbing length as far as he could into the female below him.

He was almost out of his mind with the need to possess and mark the female he knew was his. His mind was still a tortured haze of images from the past week. But in the recesses of it, a soft calming voice called to him. He recognized her scent, her touch.

When he saw his female flying backwards from the blow one of the guards had given her, his mind had splintered into a red haze of death and destruction. He would have killed everyone in the room if not for the man with the glowing amber eyes. He remembered him.

The man had grabbed him, forcing him back against the wall in an unbreakable hold as he had struggled to get at the two remaining figures still living in the room. The man had spoken to him quietly over and over. Telling him that his mate needed him. Telling him to fight the drugs and to care for his mate. Only think of his mate, nothing else but his mate.

The man had slowly released him and taken a cautious step backwards. Jazin had shoved the man further away from him and hurried to Star's crumbled body. The other male hovering over her moved away as Jazin approached, telling him that she was merely unconscious from having the breath knocked out of her.

He had growled softly at the three remaining figures, warning them away. His eyes followed as the two males helped the other female who was injured stand again. He gently pulled the small body into his arms and cradled it against him as he stood.

He had followed the others simply because he had to get his mate to safety. They had charged out into the dark night. In the center of the courtyard, a starship suddenly appeared as if out of thin air. Yells and laser fire followed them, but additional fighters appeared over the walls, forcing those who were attacking them to retreat. He never let go of the female in his arms.

His body bowed protectively around hers as he ascended the lowered platform. Even once aboard, he held her close refusing to release her as they took off under the protective fire of the fighters. The starship had burst through the atmosphere where it was escorted to a huge warship.

He had refused to leave the starship, though once it was safely docked inside the larger ship. It had only been the assurance of the male with the glowing eyes and Dakar that it would be better to leave him and Star sealed inside until the medication had passed through his system. Dakar feared if they tried to remove either Jazin or Star at this point it would cause more harm than good.

Jazin had glared at everyone until the platform sealed behind them. Only when the lights dimmed and silence surrounded him did he rise out of the seat he had taken. He searched the small starship until he found a long, narrow room with a small bunk in it.

He had gently laid the slight figure down before turning and sealing the door to the room. He would kill anyone who tried to enter and take the female from him. Once his mind registered he and the female were safe, he moved back to the bed where she lay peacefully.

His eyes roamed over her possessively. He bent over her and gripped the front of her shirt, ripping it open. His already accelerated pulse surged as a hot wave of desire sent blood flowing to his cock which throbbed painfully. Her small breasts gleamed in the muted light of the cabin.

His eyes swept down to tight, form-fitting leggings she wore. He curled his fingers around each side and pulled them down until he reached the small, soft brown boots she was wearing. With a growl of frustration, he pulled each boot off and tossed them over his shoulder. He wanted her naked, now! With another jerk, her leggings followed her boots. A low rumble escaped as her scent caressed him, begging him to take what was his.

Jazin quickly ripped the tattered pants from his waist and climbed onto the bed next to the still figure.

He wanted to see her eyes again. He wanted her to wake and accept his claim. He pulled her legs apart and settled between them before bending over to capture one of the taut peaks in his mouth. He sucked deeply on it, pulling and tugging at it mercilessly before letting it go with a loud pop in the quiet room. His body reacted violently when the small figure trapped beneath him arched in response, seeking his hot lips and tongue.

His eyes blazed with triumph before he turned his attention to the other rosy nipple begging for his attention. He sucked deeply before catching it between his teeth and biting down hard enough to pull a gasp from the soft lips.

He lowered one of his hands so he could slide his fingers into her, testing to see if she was ready. Pre-cum pearled on the tip of his cock as his fingers slid against the slickness of her hot channel. He pushed in as far as he could while sucking on her distended nipples. He pulled almost all the way out before he pressed in even harder, deeper than before.

Her light blue eyes flew open as a moan was wrenched from deep inside her. He pulled his fingers out to grip his hard length, aligning it as he rose above her to grip her hips. He wanted her to know he was claiming her. The deep, primitive haze in his mind wanted to brand her as his for all to see.

"Mine!" He roared out as he thrust his hips forward, impaling her, stretching her tight channel until they were one being, one soul.

"Jazin!" Star cried out reaching up to grip his forearms tightly as he thrust forward into her.

Star lifted her legs, winding them around Jazin's narrow hips as he pulled back and thrust forward again and again. It was as if he wanted to absorb her body into his in a fierce possession that rocked her to her soul. Emotions of relief, love, and a need to show him how much he meant to her shattered any restraints she had.

She had come so close to losing him. The first few days when she thought she lost him had made her realize what life without him would be like. She never wanted to feel that way again. She didn't think she would be able to survive if she ever lost him again.

A fist wrapped in her hair as he lowered his body closer to hers so he could push in deeper with each thrust. His heavy breath and the sounds of his grunts echoed in the room as he rocked harder and faster into her. Star released her grip around his waist, opening further to him as he became rougher in his need.

Her hushed cries became louder as the friction inside her increased and she neared the edge of the precipice she was on. Jazin jerked on the hair he had clenched in his fist, pulling her head to one side before he bit down on her shoulder. Star shattered under his assault. Her body exploding in a climax built on fear, need, and love. She arched into him as a strangled scream ripped from her throat, driving him so deep she couldn't tell where she began and he ended. Her pussy clenched his cock tightly, pulsing as her climax wrapped around him.

"You are mine!" His strangled cry echoed with her soft sobs as he ripped his mouth away from her shoulder and poured himself deep into her. His cock straining and jerking as his seed poured from him into her womb. "You are mine. I, Jazin Ja Kel Coradon of the House of Kassis, claim you, Star, for my house and as my mate. I claim you as my woman. No other may claim you. I will kill any other who try. I give you my protection as is my right as leader of my house. I claim you as is my right by the House of Kassis."

Jazin wasn't sure where the words came from. His mind could not process enough rational thought yet to understand where the words originated from. He just knew the words that poured from his mouth were as much a part of him as the breath he drew into his straining body.

He shivered as the small hands moved up over the healed flesh of his back and side before sliding up along his chest. He stared down into the light blue eyes. Confusion clouded his eyes for a moment before they filled with heat again. He crushed his lips to her swollen ones even as his body began rocking back and forth again. The adrenaline coursing through him caused his arms to tighten around her as a painful wave of intense need broke over his heated flesh.

"More," he growled in a low, deep voice. "I need more."

Star gasped as he suddenly withdrew from her and flipped her over until she was lying face down on the bed. Her gasp turned to a startled cry when his arm wrapped around her and pulled her up onto her knees while the other hand pushed her head down. He used his thick thighs to push her legs further apart, exposing her to him in a submissive position that left her vulnerable.

"Jazin," Star whispered in uncertainty.

"Hush," he hummed as he ran his hands down over her rounded ass, squeezing them. "Beautiful," he murmured before he bent over and nipped one cheek.

"Oh!" Star started in surprise.

A loud slap sounded in the quiet room as he brought his hand down on the cheek he just bit. "Don't move," he snarled in a low, husky voice. "Mine."

"Jazin?" Star whispered in a quivering voice as she felt his hand moving up and down over her ass before he spread her open. "What are you...." Her voice faded as another slap heated her other cheek.

"Quiet," he said again.

A shuddered ripped through Star but she remained silent. She trusted Jazin, even in his drug induced state. It might be crazy, but she knew he would never hurt her, no matter what. He seemed more curious. She was too. They had only had the one night together before this and he had been very gentle with her.

A part of her wanted him to lose control and take her in a wild abandonment. She had a feeling she was about to discover just how wild and abandoned he could be. A moan escaped her as she felt his searching fingers pull the lips of her pussy apart. His fingers ran up and down over the swollen folds until she felt like screaming as heat followed each and every stroke. When he curled his fingers in the soft curls and tugged, she couldn't remain silent any longer.

"Jazin, please," she moaned, burying her face in the covers of the bed.

A sharp smack followed her plea followed by another and another. Sometimes they were on her ass, other times on her swollen lips until she was almost sobbing in frustration. Just when she was about to break down, he stopped and slid his fingers into her pulsing folds. She was so wet the insides of her thighs were drenched with her need. She would have been embarrassed, if not for the fact that she was almost out of her mind with need. She didn't care what he did to her as long as he took the painful ache away.

Long fingers moved through the moisture dragging it up until he circled the tight ring of her ass. She stiffened in resistance, but he leaned over her back and flicked the tender nipple of her left breast in warning. She forced her head down and bit her lip. His cock beat against her ass in tempo with the caress of his finger as it moved back and forth over her dark channel.

She wasn't sure what he would do next. She shivered as she thought of how large he was. Her breathing escalated as she felt the tip of his cock pressing against the soft folds of her channel. She breathed a sigh of relief that changed to a cry of startled pleasure and pain as he pushed forward into her pussy at the same time as pressed his thick finger into her anus.

"You will take me here next," he murmured as he began moving both his cock and his finger together. "Yes, I will claim you every way."

Star shattered again as her body answered him. Her mind was gone. All thoughts dissolved in the heated friction of pleasure, pain and euphoria.

Chapter 14

Jazin's eyes slowly opened. His brain was clear of the confusing rush of thoughts, images, and uncontrollable urges. His body was in a state of utter contentment. He let his eyes roam the small room. He recognized the room in the starship immediately as the one he and Jarmen had worked on modifying. A frown creased his brow as he tried to remember how he ended up on it.

His last cognitive memory was of Star holding him as he slid to the floor of his prison cell. He turned his head as a soft sigh sounded in his ear. Star's hair was everywhere. It was flowing over his chest, across his shoulder and covered half of her face. His arm tightened around the warm body pressed against him. His frown turned into a groan as he remembered Dakar saying he was going to attach a Fast Patch to him.

Jazin ran his hand down over his chest and stomach feeling the smooth, tight skin. He stared blindly up at the ceiling as other images began to form as his memory slowly returned.

He remembered the uncontrollable fear and rage when he saw Star's small body flying through the air to land in a crumpled heap on the hard floor. He was aware of every breath she struggled to inhale and the need to kill everyone in the room so he could get to her.

He shuddered as he remembered Jarmen holding him back. He owed his friend so much. He had prevented him from killing Dakar and Madas. He had no doubt in his mind that he would have without a second thought. Only Jarmen was strong enough to hold him back with the drug flowing through his system.

He also remembered what he had done after they had landed. He wasn't sure where they were but he knew they must be safe. Jarmen and Dakar would have never left him if they had been worried about their safety and he knew Madas would protect Star with her life. He groaned as the vivid memories of what he had done to his little mate flowed through his now clear mind.

No wonder I feel so good, he thought with a small part of self-disgust and a huge part of awe.

She had given right back to him. She never turned away from him or protested when he took her over and over every way possible. She had submitted to him while at the same time demanding more. Her cries of passion echoed throughout the cabin mixed with his own hoarse yells as they came together time after time in a fierce, primitive mating that shook him to the bottom of his soul.

"Jazin," Star's drowsy voice murmured. "I love you so much."

He rolled over onto his side so he could look into her sleepy eyes. He pushed her tangle of blond hair back from her face with trembling fingers. His heart clenched at the thought of losing her. He pressed a kiss to her forehead and pulled her closer until her head was tucked under his chin so she couldn't see the tears burning in his eyes.

"I love you more, my little warrior," he responded huskily. "I love you more than life itself."

"I don't ever want to go through that again," she sniffed. "I thought I had lost you and I didn't want to go on. Don't ever leave me," she whispered before burying her face in his neck.

Jazin's heart twisted as he felt her warm, salty tears against his throat. He knew exactly what she meant. He would never forget the feelings coursing through him at the thought of never seeing her again. His heart felt like it was ripping apart and the pain of his torture was nothing compared to the pain at the thought of losing her.

"I won't leave you," he promised softly, holding her tightly against him. "I felt you there, with me," he whispered in awe.

"I felt you too," she sighed. "I dreamed I was touching you and when I woke there was blood on my fingers. Jazin," she paused taking a deep breath and pulling back so she could stare into his eyes.

Jazin smiled gently and threaded his fingers through a long length of her hair before resting his palm against her cheek. "What, my love?" He asked distractedly.

Star bit her swollen bottom lip and winced. She ran her the tip of her tongue over it instead. She was sore in quite a few places if she admitted it, but it was a good kind of sore.

"I saw us…. in another lifetime," she admitted. "It was so real. There were these strange creatures. They were destroying everything. I saw you battling them on a hill. There was blood everywhere. You were dressed differently, but it was you. Then, I saw huge ships appearing over where you were fighting and thousands of fighters appeared in the sky. They helped you fight against the creatures. After it was over....," she paused again to take a deep breath as the vivid memory of the blood soaked fields filled her mind. "After it was over a fighter landed and a woman got out. It was me, but it wasn't me," she whispered in confusion. "It was like I was seeing us, but it wasn't us at the same time."

Jazin drew in a deep, shuddering breath. She was describing the first meeting between his ancestor and the Goddess he would claim as his mate. He had read the account a million times in his youth wondering if he would ever find a mate like the first Jazin had. He had sworn if he ever did, he would claim her and never let her go, just as his predecessor did.

"It was us," he replied in a husky voice. "In another lifetime, but it was us."

Star leaned up on one elbow and looked deeply into his eyes. Her fingers came up and traced his brow before sliding down over his cheekbones to tenderly touch his lips. A smile played on her red, swollen lips drawing his eyes to them greedily. He tried to force his body not to respond, knowing she had to be too sore, considering how many times, not to mention ways, he had taken her. He forced his eyes back to hers and moaned softly when he saw the responding desire in them.

"I'm glad we are getting another chance," she declared. "One lifetime would never be enough to show you how much I love you."

Jazin's moan turned into a passionate groan as she replaced her fingers with her lips. He rolled her over onto her back, caging her beneath him as he took possession of her once again. He closed his eyes as he felt her closing tightly around him.

"You are right," he said hoarsely as he began rocking faster. "I am not even sure two lifetimes will be enough."

* * *

"You look fine," Jazin said as he watched Star dress in the clothes he finally had to request for her.

She was so short and tiny that none of the pants on board the starship would fit. They swallowed her petite frame. She was going to just wear one of Jarmen's shirts that had been left on board. It covered her all the way to her knees, but she looked so damn sexy in it that Jazin refused to let her off the starship.

It was probably a good thing when she thought about how he had proved his point. She had to step back into the cleansing unit for another shower when she found herself bent over the table with the tail of the shirt twisted around her waist and him buried balls deep inside her again. She was lucky she was even able to walk after all the love making they had done.

Jazin had started to apologize for his rough behavior while he was under the influence of the Fast Patch. Star had nipped that in the bud. She threatened to put another one on him if he said one more word! She had absolutely no complaints, not even if she was deliciously sore. The sparkle of mischief and sincerity must have made him believe her because he grinned wickedly as he promised he didn't need the drug to take her like he had before.

"Do you know how Madas is?" Star asked as she slid her feet into the soft leather boots she had bought. "Oh, by the way, you are going to have a bill delivered for some revenge shopping that River and I did while you were gone."

"Revenge shopping?" Jazin growled. "Who took you shopping? You were not supposed to leave the West House."

Star straightened up and put her hands on her hips. "Oh no you don't, big boy. We are so not going there again. River and I snuck out and went to town. We had a marvelous time shopping and spending your credits so just suck it up and accept it. I will not be placed on a damn pedestal. I will come and go as I please. If you don't like it...." Her voice faded when Jazin strode forward quickly and captured her lips with his own.

"I may not like it," he said huskily as he pulled back from her. "But, I will learn to accept that you are my mate. A warrior in your own right."

He did not tell her he had talked to Jarmen and Dakar while she was in the cleansing room this last time. They gave him an abbreviated version of what happened back at the fortress. The fact that he wanted to kill them for letting his mate do such a dangerous thing was overridden by his respect of what she had done. She had proven she was a true warrior.

He found out Dakar had taken a blade to his side. He had just been released from medical a short time ago. Dakar joked that Jarmen wanted to stay with him in medical just so he could avoid being around anyone else. Ajaska and Torak had finally taken pity on the man and given him his own cabin so he could hide.

Madas had been healed, but it was Gril that needed to be sedated. He had gone nuts when he saw the two warriors carrying his wounded mate. He had snatched Madas out of their arms yelling at the top of his voice for the Tearnat healer he had brought on board the warship with him. They had not been seen since she was released from the medical unit.

"Madas is with her mate," Jazin said, sliding his hand down to snare her fingers between his own. "She was wounded but the Tearnat healer has already released her. Dakar has also been released and Jarmen can heal himself."

"I liked him," Star said as they left the starship. "He was just a sweetheart and if not for him and Madas, we would never have known that you were still alive."

Jazin's fingers tightened jealously around Star's slender ones briefly before he let out his breath. "I can never repay him for his help. I had been left chained to the wall with weights attached to each arm. It was only a matter of time before I could no longer hold them and it would have grievously wounded me to the point that not even the Fast Patch could have helped me."

Star tucked her head as tears burned her eyes. Tears of sorrow for the pain Jazin had to endure, but they were mostly tears of rage at the man who had inflicted it. If she ever got the chance to kill Tai Tek she would do so without a second thought. She would never, ever let him hurt Jazin again.

"I will never let him hurt you again either," Jazin said, stopping in the middle of the landing bay and turning her toward him. Her softly mumbled vow reminding him that he was not the only one that Tai Tek had harmed. "He will not be given another chance to harm my family. We will hunt him down. I will no longer wait for him to strike next."

"I agree," Ajaska said harshly as he studied his youngest son. Pride and respect for the warrior he had grown into shone from his eyes.

"Ajaska!" Star cried out happily.

Ajaska's laughter echoed through the landing bay causing the warriors working there to stop and smile as the tiny female warrior flew into his open arms with an infectious laugh. She giggled as he tossed her up into the air and caught her again. She held onto his broad shoulders and gave him a kiss on his cheek earning a low growl of warning from Jazin. Ajaska laughed again at his son's show of possessive jealousy.

"If you were not so young and mated to my own son I would claim you as my mate. As it is, I am proud to call you my little daughter," Ajaska chuckled as he set her back onto her feet.

Jazin reached out, pulling her back into his arms the moment she was free. "You'll have to find your own mate, father," he answered with a reluctant smile.

"From what I heard, he had three of them at one time," Torak responded.

"Torak!" River scolded fiercely. "You shouldn't be telling about that."

Ajaska's face actually turned a dull red at the reminder of his youthful indiscretion. Star would have persisted if it hadn't been for the fact she was so happy to see River again. "River!" Star cried out tearfully.

River broke away from Torak's possessive arms and stepped into Star's, holding her like she never wanted to let her go. "I know how you feel now. It was horrible when we almost lost you, but at least I was with you. I was terrified the whole time you were gone," River sniffed out as she embraced Star.

Jazin fought back the desire to pull Star back into his arms as long as he could. He finally reached a thick arm around her waist and tugged gently to let her know he needed her. Perhaps he wasn't quite as normal as he thought. He could actually feel a nervousness come over him from not touching her.

"It will become more controllable," Torak murmured quietly to him. "I still have that reaction with River but it is a little more manageable than it was."

Jazin watched with a raised eyebrow when his older brother pulled River closer after she moved to walk with his father. Torak glanced sheepishly at his younger brother and shrugged. Jazin bit back a grin. He wondered if Manota was having the same reaction to Jo as he and Torak were having to her sisters. If so, he could imagine Manota going nuts. His middle brother had always been the loner out of the three of them. He liked to be left alone so he could tinker on his toys.

"I want to see Madas," Star said, startling him out of his reverie.

"She is resting at the moment," Torak called out from behind her.

Ajaska chuckled. "I seriously doubt that, but she will be once Gril gets done with her."

"He won't hurt her will he?" Star asked concerned. "She was the one who told us that Jazin was still alive. If not for her, we would never have known. If he hurts her, I'll roast his ass," she said fiercely, trying to turn around.

"Rest easy, little warrior," Ajaska said with a chuckle. "Gril would never hurt his mate. He is merely making sure she is well cared for and checking to make sure she doesn't have any injuries the healer might have missed."

Star opened her mouth to argue, but Jazin leaned down and whispered softly in her ear. Her face turned a bright, bright red before she let out a small 'Oh'. Jazin chuckled at her wide-eyed stare. Star ducked her head, letting her hair cover her burning face. It would seem that Gril was giving Madas a thorough checkup.

* * *

Later that night, Star sat in the officer's lounge with River and Madas while Ajaska, Torak and Gril met with Jazin, Dakar, Armet, and Jarmen in the commander's conference room. Star and River were about to argue with the men, but Madas had gently taken both of their arms in her larger hands and pulled them away. Star looked at her friend who seemed to be a little darker green than before.

"Madas, are you okay?" Star asked as they each sat curled up on a couch with a cup of hot tea. "You look a little greener than before."

Madas blushed a darker shade of green, tan, and red and lowered her lashes. "Gril was very upset that I was wounded," she began hesitantly.

Star sat forward with a fierce scowl on her face. "He didn't hurt you, did he?" She demanded.

"No, no..." Madas stammered before she looked up with a small grin pulling on her thin lips. "He was just concerned. He wanted to make sure I was not hurt and...." Her voice faded as she looked out of the viewport window. "I am expecting.... I did not know."

Star looked blankly at her friend for a moment. River stood up and gave Madas a huge hug. Madas sighed deeply, looking down at her folded hands grasping the mug of tea.

"You could have lost your baby because of me," Star choked out as she thought of how close they came to dying.

Madas shook her head. "I knew we would live. We have too much to live for. Tai Tek could never take that away from us."

"Madas," River said quietly, grasping her friend's hands tightly between her own. "I know this will never replace Trolis but I am happy for you."

Madas leaned forward and rested her smooth cheek against River's for a moment before she pulled back. "While I claimed Trolis as my son, he was not from my egg. Gril had two sons from a previous mating. His mate betrayed him for another shortly after the eggs hatched. It was later learned Trolis was not his true son, but he raised him as if he was. His first son, Kali, is his. They look very much alike and he is a joy. While we have been together for many years, I have never conceived. The females in my species have to reach a certain age before we become fertile. I was approaching the age, but didn't realize I had reached it as yet."

Star giggled. "Are you telling me you were still too young to have kids?"

Madas nodded. "I am considerably younger than Gril. He is two hundred and thirty-five years old while I am only seventy. Females do not normally reach breeding age until they are almost one hundred."

"You are seventy?" River asked in disbelief.

"I wished I could look that good at seventy," Star grumbled under her breath. "So, how old were you when Gril captured you?"

"He captured her?" River asked stunned. She looked at Madas with a huge grin on her face. "You have got to tell me about it."

Madas chuckled. "I was a mere forty-five when he captured me. That was one reason my mother and the clan was so upset about his claiming. As far as they were concerned, I was still a child. But I wasn't," she added. "I knew the moment I saw him that he was my mate."

"I thought you said he was the ugliest male you had ever seen when you first saw him," Star said confused.

"I did and he was. That does not mean that I did not realize he was my mate," Madas said primly. "Why do you think I fought him so hard?"

All three women burst into laughter as they shared their first impressions, frustrations, and funniest times with their chosen mates. That was how the men found them later that evening. Gril was the first to snatch Madas up and whisk her away despite her weak protests. Torak was next. He pulled River into his arms, ignoring her protests that she was getting too big for him to carry her around everywhere. Finally, it was just Jazin and Star. He sat down next to her for a few minutes, not saying anything but enjoying the peace and quiet as he held her close to his heart.

"What about Tai Tek?" Star finally asked, breaking the silence.

"We go after him. He escaped through a new tunnel that was not on the original map of the fortress," Jazin said quietly.

"When?" She asked with a shiver.

"Jarmen, Dakar and Armet are running calculations on where they think he might go next. It is time we were on the offensive," he responded carefully.

"Where do we even start?" She asked, looking up into Jazin's eyes. There was something he wasn't telling her.

Jazin sighed heavily before he scooped Star up into his arms. "We start on Elpidios."

Chapter 15

Elpidios: Two weeks later

Commander Mena Rue stood at attention. It was not that hard to do really. She was frozen with fear. The Grand Ruler sat in the seat on the other side of the desk from her, but he could just have as easily been holding a blade to her throat.

She swallowed again as bile rose, threatening to choke her. She had not only returned to Elpidios with no crystals, but she had returned with a tale so huge, so ludicrous she would be surprised if the officers she left outside the room were not ordered in to remove what was left of her body. The Grand Ruler was not someone you wanted angry at you. He was not only angry at Mena, he was beyond furious as he looked back down at her report.

"Do you really expect me to believe this," he growled out in a low, dangerous tone.

Inwardly, Mena cringed. Outwardly, she remained completely at attention with a blank mask on her face. She swallowed and nodded once, unable to force the words out that would condemn her to instant death.

"Do you?" He snapped as he threw down the report and stood up to glare at her.

"Yes, sir," Mena choked out.

"Why?" He asked, turning to look out over his dying world.

"My parents studied the ancient archives. They are known for their research," Mena began.

"I am well aware of everything about you, Commander Rue. Including who your parents are and what they do," the Grand Ruler snapped out without turning around. "I want to know why you think this female is a messenger for an ancient prophesy that was written over two thousand years ago."

"The ancient tablets my parents found when I was younger spoke of the first sign that would tell of the coming of the great Empress. It spoke of a strange pale skinned female with eyes the color of the Elpidios oceans. The female is said to be one of three great warriors who will save the House of Kassis and bring forth the future Empress of Elpidios. Through the bond of these great females will come the lifesaving blood stones that will save Elpidios, its people and its world," Mena said passionately as she retold the tale told to her over and over by her parents as they struggled to find a way to save their dying planet.

"We already know what we need to save our world," the Grand Ruler stated coldly, turning to look at Mena with a relentlessness that had her taking a step backwards. "Do you truly believe in this myth that was written thousands of years ago?"

"She is the first sign," Mena insisted in an unsteady voice. "It is said she will bring your bride."

And that, thought Risteárd Roald, *was the problem.*

He was not looking for a bride and when he did, it would not be to any alien female from an obscure prophecy. Rage built inside him as the strange feeling of helplessness swept through him. His father and his father before him for countless generations had searched for a solution to the radiation slowly killing their world. It was caused by the thinning of their atmosphere. It was a phenomenon that had happened once before almost causing the extinction of his race. His ancestors had no choice before, but to live in the great underground cities beneath their soil.

Over time, their world had returned to normal. It was said that a deadly species had come to attack their world only to die themselves in massive numbers due to the radiation. It was their blood that had spilled into the soil, giving the life-giving crystals that had kept their world safe for almost two thousand years. The crystals had kept their planet alive, but several generations of illegal gathers had depleted the source of the crystals until none remained.

His grandfather had discovered what was happening and had tried to stop the sale of the crystals, but he had been murdered by the very council ordained to protect his ruling and their planet. His father had executed the traitors and became the first Grand Ruler. He had spent his life and energy devoted to the research to find a way to save their world.

Elpidios scientists worked tirelessly on solutions, both through the study of their history and through extensive research. It had finally been determined that there was another source of the crystals. A small amount of Kassisan crystal had been purchased and it matched the crystals from their world.

His world needed the crystals to power the shield generators that would create a protective grid around their planet. The problem was they needed a huge quantity of it until they could grow the crystals on their own. His scientists had successfully been able to do so, but they could not grow them fast enough at this point to save his people. Ristéard would have to approach Ajaska Ja Kel Coradon. If the Kassis ruling family denied his request, he would have to weigh whether to attack or just steal the necessary crystals. Either way did not bode well for his people.

The com on his desk sounded. Ristéard gave the command to open communications.

"Grand Ruler, a Kassisan warship is hailing the planet. Lord Ajaska Ja Kel Coradon is asking for permission to meet with you," the voice on the other end stated.

"Patch me through to him," Ristéard ordered without turning around. "Get out," he added to Mena.

It would appear his meeting was going to take place sooner than he expected. He would see if what Commander Rue was speculating could be true. And it if was, then he would deal with the consequences. In the meantime, he needed to convince a species he knew very little about to give him a large quantity of their power source.

"Yes, sir," Mena said stiffly with a salute before turning sharply and exiting the room.

"How did it go?" Her second in command asked as soon as she closed the door behind her.

Mena leaned back against the closed door and released the shaky breath that she had been holding. "Better than I expected," she responded looking at her friend with a tired smile. "I'm still alive."

* * *

Jazin looked down on the planet through the conference room viewport. His father had contacted the Elpidios Grand Ruler and they were to meet within the next hour. They had all been surprised when the Grand Ruler asked them to bring the pale alien female with them. Torak had argued that his mate did not need to go. They did not know enough about the Elpidios to expose their mates to such danger, especially with her expecting.

Ajaska was hesitant but the Grand Ruler insisted that if the pale alien was not part of the landing party they would be denied permission to land. It had taken Gril, Ajaska and finally River to assure Torak that everything would be fine. The Grand Ruler gave his word that all he wanted was to meet her.

What Jazin didn't like was the fact that Star would be traveling with them as well. Of course, as soon as Madas heard the other women were going she informed them she wasn't about to be left behind. Jazin decided it was in his best interest to keep his mouth shut after listening to Torak and Gril. Especially when Star gave him 'the look' and calmly informed him to 'not even think about it'.

"Everything will be okay," Star said quietly.

He had been so lost in thought he had not even heard the conference room door open. He turned and smiled reassuringly at his mate. She was so beautiful. She was wearing a soft, light blue shirt tucked into a pair of form-fitting pants and the soft brown boots she was so proud of. He made a mental note to buy her a dozen pairs in every color available. Opening his arms, he chuckled when she hurried forward and snuggled up to him.

"I love you, my little warrior," he murmured, pressing a kiss to the top of her head.

"You know, this is really exciting," Star exclaimed, leaning back a little so she could stare out the viewport window.

Jazin frown. "What is?"

"Seeing other worlds and meeting new people," she said with a grin. "That is the thing I missed the most when Jo and I left the circus. We met new people in Orlando but it wasn't the same. When we traveled with the circus, we got to see new things all the time. Especially once Walter and Nema decided to take it worldwide," she sighed as she turned in his arms and leaned back against his chest. "I wonder how Jo is doing. I miss her so much."

A chuckle sounded from behind them. Jazin's head turned at the sound and he frowned. That was the second time in as many seconds that he had been taken by surprise. He shook his head in disgust. Ever since his capture he had been having trouble keeping his thoughts on the task at hand.

Correction, he thought as he breathed in the heady scent of his mate. *Ever since I met a certain alien female I've had problems keeping my mind on the matters at hand.*

"Your sister is doing well," Ajaska said with a grin. "I am not so sure how well my son is doing though."

"What do you mean?" Star asked surprised. "Are Jo and Manota fighting?"

"No, they are not fighting," Ajaska replied as he came to stand next to them and stare down at the planet far below. "It would appear your parents are not the only travelers returning with your sister and my son."

"Oh. My. God!" River squealed from the door as she came rushing into the room. "Star, Walter, Nema, Ricki, and the whole circus are coming!"

River danced over to Star with a huge grin on her face. Torak came in shortly behind her with a pained expression on his. Star's mouth dropped open before it snapped shut and she squealed in return, locking hands with River and dancing around in a circle.

"Do you think this is some type of ritual?" Jazin asked his father and brother as the two women squealed, giggled, and talked in broken sentences that only they appeared to understand.

"I am not sure our planet is ready for this," Torak growled out in a low tone. "Do you remember the vids we watched? What if those clowns get loose? You saw the damage they could do."

Ajaska chuckled. He had no idea what would happen to his world when this 'circus' arrived but he would bet everything he had that life was about to get even more interesting than it had been.

He glanced at the resignation on the faces of his eldest and youngest sons' faces. Vivid emotions flickered across each one. For a brief moment, Ajaska thought about what it would be like to have a mate like the two females who were talking in rapid, breathless sentences as they shared stories. Their faces glowed with an internal beauty and energy making them appear almost ethereal. He could easily understand what his ancestors must have thought when they first saw the unusual beauty and strength of the alien females from long ago.

"Father?" Jazin asked again with a bemused frown on his face, touching his father's arm to draw his attention back to the present.

Ajaska jerked out of his reverie. "Yes?"

"The shuttle is ready. Gril and Madas will be joining us as well," Jazin said carefully.

"Of course," Ajaska said, clearing his throat as he glanced briefly at River and Star who were still talking as they trailed Torak out of the conference room before he followed as well.

Jazin didn't say anything. He had seen the look of envy in his father's eyes. He had never thought about the fact that his father might be lonely. It had been so long ago that his mother had passed to the next world that he could barely remember her at times. She had been given to his father in a bid to heal a rift between his clan and the clan of a distant cousin. He knew his father had never loved his mother but he had been good to her. He knew that from conversations with his father's man, Je'zi, who now served Torak and River. His father had poured everything he had into protecting his people. The war had taken a lot out of his father and he still bore the mark of it on his face.

Jazin trailed slowly behind the others, deep in thought. His life had changed so much since his capture the first time. His eyes moved over the slim figure of his mate as she chatted with River. He almost grimaced at how fast his body reacted to that simple gaze. His cock swelled with the memory of their lovemaking.

Gods, everything about her heats my blood, he thought fiercely.

He knew one thing, the Grand Ruler better be a man of his word because if he tried to harm one hair on his mate or River he would kill the male without a second thought. He was tired of those who thought they could harm him, his mate, or his family. It was time to end this once and for all.

* * *

Ristéard stood at the edge of the landing platform watching as the Kassisan shuttle slowed for landing. He was an imposing sight. At close to seven feet of pure muscle, he carried an air of barely suppressed violence in his stance.

His light blue skin was swirled with darker blue tattoos that he wore proudly. He had earned each in either battle or competition against those who thought to take his title. Those who were stupid enough to dare either one died a slow, painful death.

He did not show mercy to anyone, be they male or female. There had been three females who thought to take his place, one in battle, two by deceit. He had killed them as slowly as he had killed the numerous males who had tried. If they wished to cause him harm, he felt they deserved the same punishment.

His people knew he could be a brutal, heartless warrior, but they also knew he was a fair ruler who gave to them. His research showed Lord Ajaska Ja Kel Coradon, Leader of Kassis, was the same.

After he was informed that Ja Kel Coradon wanted to meet with him, he had ordered Commander Rue to return. He had wanted to know everything she knew about the Leader of Kassis.... everything. He could tell by the increase in her breathing and the flush to her skin that she was withholding information from him at first.

His softly hissed command warned her not to hold anything back if she valued not only her position but her life. She told him of the night she and two other officers had spent with the leader almost forty years before when they had just completed training and were partying on a distant Spaceport. She relayed what she remembered in specific detail.

Her insight to that night gave him an idea of the type of male he would be facing. It had also left him highly aroused which was a constant state for an Elpidios male. After he had dismissed her, he had called for one of the women he kept for his pleasure. As he bent her over his desk, taking his time with her, his mind focused on the information he had. His release came swiftly, taking the edge off, but never satisfying him. He pushed the disappointment to the back of his mind. He had more important things to deal with than the constant hunger that ate at him. After the female cleaned him, he dismissed her back to the rooms where the females he kept for his private use lived without another thought.

Now, he was focused solely on the pale skinned female that Commander Rue said was the first sign of the prophesy stating his bride, the female who would save his world, was coming. The shuttle landed and within moments the platform opened, allowing the passengers to disembark.

Ristéard's eyebrow lifted when he saw the huge figure of a Tearnat male walk down the platform first and look around with a deep scowl on his face. He stared intently at Ristéard for a moment before he dipped his head in respect. Only when Ristéard responded in kind did he motion for the others. A slender, darker green Tearnat female walked down the platform with her head held high. Ristéard bit back a smile at the scowl the huge Tearnat gave the female who waved her hand at him as if brushing away an annoying speck. She stepped off the platform and turned to stand next to the male who immediately wrapped a huge arm around her waist, drawing her protectively against him.

The next one down the platform was a huge male that could only be Ajaska Ja Kel Coradon from Commander Rue's description. He was almost as big as Ristéard, both in height and in strength from the look of it. He paused, looking over at Ristéard before he looked up the platform and nodded.

Ristéard's attention was truly caught at the protectiveness of the males for those who were still aboard the shuttle. He understood why the moment he saw the next two couples descending. His eyes were riveted to the two beautiful females descending the platform, surrounded by four males who searched the area intensely for any signs of a threat.

The females had golden, pale skin. Their coloring and size contrasted each other as if they had been painted with two different brushes by two different artists. One was taller, with dark hair hanging in a long braid down her slender back.

When she glanced at him, he could see that her eyes were indeed the color of their oceans. The dark, dark blue that pulled at the soul of the searcher. His eyes roamed her sleek form pausing on the slight swell of her abdomen. His eyes moved to the slightly taller male who glared back at him in warning.

Her mate, Ristéard thought. *He would not be an easy adversary to beat.*

Ristéard bowed his head slightly in acknowledgement of the male's warning. He would give him the respect of knowing he would not harm another's mate unless it was necessary. He held sacred the bond between mates and a female while she was breeding.

His eyes moved to the other female who fascinated him with her unusual coloring. Commander Rue did not mention a second pale-skinned female. She was so small he might have wondered if she was a child if it had not been for the way the other male had his hand on her.

Her hair was a color he had never seen before except in the crystals that used to litter his world. The few crystals that were left had belonged to the ruling family and his father had turned them over to the scientists in the hopes they could discover the property hidden inside them. Only a handful remained. The others used up or destroyed in the experiments.

The color was so intense, he wanted to run his hands through the silky strands to see if it felt as soft as it looked. She turned and looked at him with eyes the lightest of blue. It reminded him of the color of the few infants still being born. An Elpidios infant was born a pale blue and slowly became darker as it matured.

Ristéard tilted his head in confusion as he felt another ache deep inside that he had never experienced before, as if his body was craving something that was missing. The feeling disappeared almost as soon as it appeared.

The female smiled brightly at him and waved her hand in greeting drawing a quick response from the male touching her. Her soft laughter echoed as she responded to whatever the male said. It was obvious she was not in the least intimidated by him. This confused Ristéard even more considering the female was so tiny compared to the male.

He approached the small group as the last six stepped from the platform. His small, elite guard following him at a discreet distance. He stopped in front of Ajaska, assessing him.

"Welcome to Elpidios," Risteárd said. "I am Risteárd Roald."

"I am Ajaska Ja Kel Coradon. This is Gril Tal Mod, Leader of the Tearnat and his mate, Madas," Ajaska stated calmly. "The other two are members of our security team," he continued without giving either man's name. "They will remain with the shuttle."

Risteárd ignored the two men before bowing in respect to Gril and Madas. His eyes turned to the two females standing between the other two males. "And these are?" He asked.

"My oldest son, Torak, and his mate, River Knight," Ajaska responded cautiously, not sure he liked the edge of curiosity in the Elpidios leader's voice. "The other is my youngest son, Jazin, and his mate, Star Strauss."

Risteárd took a startled step back when Star stepped forward unexpectedly and held her hand out. "Hi," she said with a bright, infectious smile lighting up her face. "I'm Star. It's a pleasure to meet you."

Risteárd's lips twitched as he noticed the slightly daring look in her eyes, as if she was challenging him to see if he would pass some secret test. When she raised an eyebrow, he found his own hand, swallowing her smaller one. She squeezed it briefly before pulling back with a small giggle. The low growl coming from the male by her side and her rolled eyes in response drew an unexpected chuckle from him.

"Welcome, Lady Star," Risteárd said with a deeper bow before he looked at her mate who took a step closer in warning. He paused before turning to address Ajaska with a calm he hadn't felt in years. "Please follow me. We have much to discuss."

Chapter 16

Ristéard escorted them to where several transports waited. He did not ride with any of them but instead sat upon what looked like a motorcycle without wheels. His elite guard rode similar types of vehicles. The transport they were escorted to was almost identical to those on Kassis.

"I want one of those," Madas said with a mischievous grin as they slipped into the transport. "They look like fun."

Gril snorted. "No."

"Have you ever ridden one?" Madas asked her mate with a raised eyebrow.

Gril flushed a darker tan. "Yes," he responded reluctantly. "But the answer is still no."

Madas stared at Gril intently until he broke eye contact with a sigh of resignation. "You are breeding. You shouldn't do anything dangerous," he muttered defensively.

Star and River giggled as the huge Tearnat fought giving in to his mate. Star loved watching Madas with her mate. They reminded her so much of her own parents. Her dad was forever trying to coddle her mother and her mother was forever driving him nuts by doing the exact opposite.

"It wouldn't be dangerous if you were on it with me," Madas purred tenderly as she laid her head down on her larger mate's chest.

Gril looked at the other men with a pained expression. "Do you see what she does to me? I lose all common sense when she wants something," he growled out.

Ajaska laughed while Torak and Jazin looked at River and Star with a mutinous expression on their faces. "Well, it does look like fun. I've ridden motorcycles before. It can't be that much different," Star said with a twinkle in her eyes.

"Absolutely….," Jazin started to say stubbornly before he noticed the teasing curve to his tiny mate's lips. "Maybe if we ride together," he grunted before he glared at Gril who was chuckling.

Twenty minutes later, they pulled into an underground area under the huge palace made of the same type of black stones of the fortress. Star shivered at the memory of it. Her eyes searched out Jazin. She let them roam over his smooth skin. He still bore the thin scar from where Progit cut him. Her eyes moved down to his bare arms. He was wearing the black leather vest, pants, and boots that she had come to recognize as being their military uniform. Ajaska and Torak were dressed the same. Her eyes lingered on the smooth skin of his shoulders and the small area of his chest that was visible. She remembered the torn flesh. If she looked close enough, she could still see a light spider web of scars where the skin healed together.

The scars were fading faster than the memories, she thought, wondering if she would ever be able to forget what Tai Tek had done to him.

"What is it?" Jazin asked quietly in her ear. "What upsets you?"

"We still don't know where Tai Tek could have gone," Star said quietly. "How are we supposed to find him if he keeps disappearing? The guy scares me, Jazin. I don't ever what him to hurt you again."

"We will find him, my little warrior," Jazin murmured in her ear as he pulled her close to him as the transport drew to a stop. "Dakar, Armet, and Jarmen are working on it. Those three can find anything. Dakar knows all of Tai Tek's hiding places and Jar, well, let us just say he has talents few others possess," he added as he let his hand slide behind her back to massage the curve of her hip.

"I hope so," she answered softly as the door opened for them to get out. "I really, really hope so."

The small group was escorted up a series of wide, polished steps. The walls of the palace were so smooth that the surface resembled a highly polished mirror. The only light came from what was reflecting down from the large windows. Star reached her hand out to touch the surface with her finger and gasped as threads of gold blossomed from where her fingers touched it. She touched it again and more strands of gold shimmered before fading.

"The stone contains a natural chemical," Ristéard's deep voice explained from the top of the staircase. "Run your hand along it."

Star looked up at the huge blue man in awe before doing as he suggested. She ran her hand in a large wave along the wall. Hundreds of gold filaments appeared, flowing outward to make brilliant designs before fading again.

"That is so awesome," Star giggled as she did it again. "River, you have got to try this!"

River and Madas reached over and ran their hands over the wall. "Okay, we're happy. You guys can go talk the boring stuff. We'll stay and play with the walls," River said as she looked over her shoulder at Torak.

"This is better than when we saw all that phosphorescence when we were crossing over to Europe that time," Star exclaimed excitedly.

Jazin, Torak and Gril each wrapped a beefy arm around their respective mates and tugged them away from the wall that had them so fascinated. They were never going to get anywhere if the giggles the females were emitting were anything to go by.

"Come, you can play with the walls another time," Jazin said with a chuckle.

All three women groaned, but followed the men as they ascended the stairs until they were even with Risteard. They followed the huge ruler down several different corridors until they came to a set of huge, solid black doors with intricate cravings etched into it. The doors must have weighed a ton because it took two warriors on each side to open them. Even then, Star could see the men's arm muscles straining to pull the doors open.

Risteard escorted them into a lavishly decorated room. Huge tapestries depicting different events covered the mirrored black walls. Along one wall, a huge fireplace stood empty. Over the mantle of it was another tapestry. The figures of two men stood side by side. One slightly older than the other. In the picture, they each held a bloody sword and the area around them was littered with the remains of dead warriors. It wasn't something Star would want hanging in her living room, but since this wasn't her house she wouldn't say anything. Instead, she continued her observation of the room.

Windows from floor to ceiling graced the west wall. Heavy curtains were pulled back with thick ropes of silver and gold. A large round table that could seat at least a dozen men sat near the center of the room. Two large, silver couches with twin matching chairs were arranged in front of the vacant fireplace. Six matching end tables made of the black stone sat at each end of the furniture.

Ristéard stood to one side as they entered. The moment Star walked by him, he reached out to touch her hair. She turned when she felt the slight tug on it, but relaxed when she saw he was looking at the strands he had gathered with a fascinated expression. She was used to people doing the same thing when the circus used to tour Asia and parts of the Middle East. Jazin carefully pulled Star away, but the Grand Ruler wasn't finished with his analysis of her hair.

He followed them into the room touching the silky wave repeatedly until Jazin reached out and gripped his wrist. A member of Ristéard's elite guard stepped forward at the violation to his ruler. Ristéard studied Jazin's taunt face for a moment before he flicked his hand, dismissing his guards.

Ristéard tilted his head ever so slightly to let Jazin know he understood the silent warning before he walked over to where Ajaska, Torak, and River sat at the end of the table. Jazin placed his hand protectively on Star's lower back and guided her away from the huge blue leader toward the two couches where Gril and Madas sat.

"What do you think of Ristéard?" She asked quietly as she sat down on the plush couch.

A low rumble escaped Jazin before he could stop it as his gaze flickered to the Elpidios ruler who was speaking intensely with his father. What did he think of the Grand Ruler? He was seriously thinking of killing the bastard! That was what he was thinking. Ristéard had taken every opportunity he could to touch Star's soft hair as they came in.

The bastard hadn't even tried to make it appear as if it was an accident. After the fifth time his hand reached out to touch a strand, Jazin had enough and gripped his wrist in warning. The male had finally moved to sit next to Ajaska but his eyes kept returning to Star's hair.

"She is a very unique female, is she not?" Ajaska asked Ristéard when he saw the male's eyes drift back to where his little daughter sat on the couch with her mate.

"My apologies," Ristéard murmured with a slight twist to his lips at the understatement. "I have never seen this color before and find it fascinating. Is it common among their species?"

River giggled as she heard the quietly spoken words and responded for Ajaska who looked to her for guidance. "It is fairly common. We have all different color hair. While mine is a dark brown, Star and Jo have an almost white-blond. Our friend Ricki has blond hair too but it is more of a honey blond. Others have black or red hair. Even those can vary greatly. The way you were reacting reminded me of the time we were in Turkey. Star, Jo, and Ricki almost didn't make it out of Istanbul. Do you remember that, Star?"

Star laughed as she nodded her head. "Ricki ended up buying head scarves for all of us so we could get out of the market without being mugged or kidnapped. The people that live in that area have dark hair like you so when they saw us it was like sending up a flashing light saying 'foreigners!'."

"There is a third female? She is a warrior like yourself?" Ristéard asked with an intense look of interest in his eyes.

"Lady Jo is my son Manota's mate," Ajaska said in quiet warning at the interest that flashed through Ristéard's eyes.

"Who is this Ricki?" Ristéard asked cautiously as a feeling of unease began to grow deep inside him.

"Ricki is the Empress of Organization!" River laughed. "If you need something done, have a challenge that seems impossible to conquer or need to find something she is the one who can do it."

"That is an understatement!" Star said with a shake of her head. "If you need a miracle she is the one to pull it off for you. I've never seen anyone accomplish some of the things she has with just a few taps of her fingers. She is pure magic."

"I hope we get to spend some time with her once she gets here," River said. "But, knowing Ricki, she'll spend the next six months researching every law and by-law in the known star systems to see what she needs to do to ease things for everyone else."

Ristéard listened as the two unusual females talked for a short time about some of the 'miracles' this Ricki had accomplished. His mind filtered through their conversation picking out key elements. From what he could gather this female was renowned for her abilities to get items no one else could and she could handle situations others found impossible.

His eyes flickered back over the two women again, noting their unusual beauty and grace. He felt his body stir with desire at the idea of having a female of his own with white hair. Perhaps it was time to add another female to his house. He wondered if they came in a larger size.

Ristéard observed the way the young Kassisan lord tightened his hold on the tiny female. While he found the tiny, light haired female fascinating she did not stir his blood sexually. She was too small. He would be afraid of breaking her. He shook his head and turned his attention back to the matters at hand.

The past two hours had been very insightful. He did not like to learn he was being manipulated. He would send his own men to find the Kassisan male who thought to use him for his own gain. It was not often that he could be fooled. His concern for his people had clouded the reservations he had at the male's promises.

"You are in agreement to supply the necessary crystals we need then?" Ristéard asked focusing back on Ajaska and Torak who had been discussing the best way to handle the increased need for the energy crystals.

"Yes." Ajaska nodded. "Torak will return to Kassis and make the necessary arrangements. We should able to supply you with the first shipment within three weeks' time."

"In the meantime, we have some reserves on board two of our warships that can be transported down to help out. Our scientists have successfully replicated the crystals. I can organize a team of researchers to come to Elpidios with your permission," Torak added.

Ristéard looked from father to son. He could see no signs of deceit on their faces or in their voices, only genuine concern. It had been so long since he had felt like he could trust another he was reluctant to believe it possible there were others out in the star system with a code of honor that matched his own.

His head jerked around when he felt a slender hand lightly touch his. "The Houses of Kassis will not let you or your people down," River said with a comforting smile. "It was hard for me to trust as well. They will stand beside you."

His dark silver eyes stared deeply into the dark blue ones of the pale-skinned female. For a moment, he was lost in their depths. He could almost see something in the swirling colors. He jerked back to the present when she withdrew her hand and nodded his head as he stood up.

"You are welcome to enjoy the hospitality of the palace. I have several meetings scheduled that I need to attend. I will make arrangements for the necessary supply ships to leave within the next few days. I would like to tour the Crystal Replication Plant you spoke of personally. I will contact you shortly with the arrangements," Ristéard stated with a quiet authority that conveyed the meeting was over.

Everyone rose from where they were sitting. Both Torak and Jazin slid their arms protectively around their mates. Ristéard turned and took a step toward Jazin and Star. Before Jazin could stop him, the Grand Ruler reached out to touch Star's hair one last time with a twisted smile.

"Unusual," he murmured before he let it go and left without another word.

Star laughed when she saw Jazin's expression. He looked for all the world like he would like to kick the huge, blue guy's ass. She squeezed his fingers to let him know he didn't have a thing to worry about before they followed the others out of the room.

Chapter 17

Three days later they were heading to a distant Spaceport on the outer rim of the Tearnat star system. Out of the dozen warships, only three remained. The *Blue Star*, Jazin's warship and two of the Tearnat warships. Gril and Madas had departed on the other Tearnat warship after Gril had received a report that there was an small uprising of rebels on his home planet.

Torak and River had returned to Kassis while Ajaska took another ship to the Dramentic star system when the Alliance council reported a disturbance on the outer edge of their system. Ajaska's heated curses could be heard as he made arrangements to leave. He took six warships with him to subdue the conflict. The last remaining Kassis warship developed engine problems and was currently still in orbit around Elpidios until the repairs could be completed.

Star frowned as she thought of all the events that just suddenly seemed to explode all at once. She wasn't the only one who thought that was unusual either. She had listened in before the others left that it was very uncommon for the Dramentic star system to have issues but a mining asteroid had been under attack. The Dramentians were a passive society who were known for their negotiating skills, not their fighting ability. That was one reason they relied heavily on the Alliance for protection. The last head chancellor of the Alliance was from the Dramentic star system. Trolis had killed him. It was during that incident that Star, Jo, and River met Jazin, Torak, and later Manota.

Jazin had been in meetings on and off for the last three days. She walked over to the replicator and programmed it for a cup of hot tea. She was just turning back to her comfy spot by the viewport to read some more when the door sounded letting her know someone was requesting permission to enter. Star was surprised since she wasn't expecting anyone. She set her cup down on the small table next to the door and waved her hand over the panel. The door slid open to reveal two men she had never seen before. One was slightly shorter than the other. The taller man wore the standard uniform of security while the shorter one wore the maintenance uniform. Star was surprised to see a small repair cart behind them.

"Jazin's not in right now," Star said, looking at them with a smile. "I can request his location if you would like. Is something broken?"

"A repair order came in for your replicator," the shorter man said.

Star turned her head and looked at the replicator she had just used. "It is working fine. I just used it," she said, turning to look at both men again with a frown.

"A work order was submitted and I have to look at it," the man insisted.

Star stepped back as a funny feeling turned her stomach. "I'll call Jazin and see if he was having problems with it," she said turning to reach for the comlink she hadn't put on since she was still in the cabin.

"That won't be necessary," the taller man said raising his arm and firing.

Both men watched as Star jerked forward, knocking the cup off the table. Her fingers curled as the shock moved through her body, clenching her muscles before darkness settled around her. The taller man entered, picking up the cup and placing it in the cleansing unit while the other man pushed the cart inside the cabin.

Within minutes, they were heading down the long corridor. They only had minutes to get the body of the female in position. Every three days, liquid waste was flushed out of the ship. This time there would be a solid mass going with it.

* * *

Jazin rubbed the back of his neck tiredly. He had been receiving reports from all over and had conferenced with his father, brother, Gril, and the Commander of the warship they had left behind at Elpidios. His father discovered the mining asteroid had been destroyed. There was nothing left of it except some chunks of metallic fragments. Whoever was responsible was long gone by the time they reached it.

Gril discovered the group of rebels were nothing more than a small group of young Tearnats that had been promised extra credits and time with some females if they caused a disruption. He was interrogating them separately, but the stories were all the same. Three older Tearnat males came to their villages with the promises of wealth and women. In exchange all they had to do was pretend to cause an uprising. They had all been told it was to help with a military training. Gril was ready to slap every single one of them into the military for some real training!

The commander of the warship left at Elpidios couldn't understand how the circuit boards had received water damage. The only way was if they had been sabotaged on purpose. He was reviewing the crew roster to see who had access to that level. The only thing that appeared to be going right was on his home planet. Torak had arrived just in time.

He had gone to one of their largest Crystal Replication Plants. During a tour of the facility he had observed several workers acting strangely. He had his elite guards stop and search the men.

Enough explosives to disable the plant and kill an untold number of workers was discovered. The men had resisted and two of the three were killed. The last one was gravely wounded.

Torak ordered all plants to undergo lock down and be thoroughly searched. All workers were to be reviewed as well. Once the worker who was injured recovered enough to speak, Torak said he would find out what other terrorist acts were planned.

"You need rest, my friend," Jar said coming to stand next to where Jazin was standing watching the men below him on the bridge.

"Soon," Jazin responded. "How far are we to where Dakar thinks Tai Tek may have taken refuge?"

"Another two days," Jar said quietly. "I am concerned with the things that have been occurring. An analysis of the events suggests they are just a distraction for something else. I have run each through several different scenarios. Only one comes up with a higher than normal percentage of acceptability."

Jazin shook his head, looking down tiredly before his lips curved in a small smile at his unusual friend. "What outcome is that?"

Jar looked at Jazin with a frown. "That it is a distraction to limit the number of warships available is obvious, but the second is to perhaps take something without it being known."

Jazin looked at his friend with a thoughtful look. He was about to ask him what he thought someone would take when the *Blue Star* rocked violently. Alarms blared as the lights flickered. Red emergency lights came on.

A second wave hit the warship tilting it upward on the port side briefly before the stabilizers kicked in. Jazin grabbed the railing around the upper level of the bridge. Jar did the same. Both men reached out to grab a warrior who reached for the railing, but missed as the second wave hit.

The male was thrown up and over, his body falling to the level below with a sickening thump. Jar held onto the back of Jazin's vest when he almost went over the railing after the male as he grabbed for him.

Shouts and moans echoed throughout the bridge as calls to extinguish the small fires and those thrown around that could still move struggled to their feet. Jazin looked at Jar who nodded to him and focused. Jar's amber eyes glowed and he began speaking rapidly.

"One of the Tearnat's warships exploded. Our shields are holding but the blast sent shockwaves through space. The other Tearnat ship was closer and it has received severe damage. Hull integrity has been compromised on the Tearnat warship on decks eight, twelve, and fifteen. Evacuation is underway. Implosion of the warship is probable. The *Blue Star*'s hull is undamaged. The engines are off-line due to the shockwave. Minor damage on decks one, five, six, ten, eleven, twenty, and twenty-two. Unknown number of casualties or injuries at this time. Emergency response teams have been activated and medical teams have been deployed. I would recommend moving eight point four-five kilometers away from the Tearnat ship to reduce further damage," Jar said as the amber light in his eyes slowly returned to normal.

"Star," Jazin muttered as he fought between his responsibility to his warship and to his mate.

"I will go check on her," Jar said as he released his grip on the railing. "I will let you know immediately."

"Thank you, my friend," Jazin said with a nod. "Tell her I would have come myself, but I have to make sure the ship is safe first."

"I will," Jar said as he stepped closer to the door. It didn't open at first. Jar gripped it at the seam and pulled it open as if he was tearing paper from a box.

Jazin looked down at the men moving below him. Two warriors were removing the body of the man who fell. The crew members, who could, were working on repairing the equipment at their stations while others were helping those who were injured.

Jazin ordered the alarms off. Lights began to flicker back on as the emergency teams worked to restore order. Jazin ordered the comlink repaired as soon as possible. They needed to rescue as many Tearnats as they could before the second warship disintegrated.

..*

Jar worked his way down to deck four. Along the way he passed several injured warriors. He paused long enough to record their location and submitted it to the emergency medical team closest to them. He was not hampered by the limitation of the communication systems as he could bypass it and patch directly into the warship's computer system. That was how he contacted Dakar and Armet.

"How long before you are able to get the systems back online?" Jar asked as he patched into their comlink.

"Us?" Dakar growled out. "You're the one with the computer brain. Why don't you just fix the damn thing?"

"I am good, but I am not that good," Jar said seriously. "I will begin bringing what systems I can online, but I do not want to override my own systems."

"We are in the landing bay. Two of the shuttles broke loose and slammed into another. It is going to take a while to get the equipment we need to pull them off the one," Armet cursed.

Jar paused for a moment before he pushed open the door to the emergency hatch leading to the lower level. "Was the Tearnat Starship damaged?"

"It sustained some minor damage when the front end of one of the shuttles hit it," Armet said. "It will take a few hours to repair, but it should be fine."

Jar grabbed the handrails on each side of the ladder leading down and slid down to the next level. "Very well. I am checking on Jazin's little warrior."

"Gods," Armet cursed again. "I didn't even think about her. Fine Captain of the Guard I am," he said in disgust. "I'm on my way up."

"I will inform her," Jar said signing off.

He walked down the corridor noticing it was empty. That was not unusual as this level contained the living quarters of some of the officers and several relaxation lounges for the crew. He stopped in front of the door to Jazin and Star's living quarters unsure of the protocol of asking for admittance when there was no automatic alert. He raised his hand and knocked loudly several times. When he didn't receive an answer, he became concerned that perhaps the little warrior had been knocked unconscious or hurt badly.

He gripped the door and pulled it open. He immediately knew she was not in the room. He stepped inside and breathed deeply. His senses immediately picked up the scent of the little female.

He also picked up the faint scent of Jazin. What concerned him was the scent of two unfamiliar males. His eyes narrowed and he scanned the room. He stopped when he came to the moisture on the floor near the door. He bent down and swiped his finger through the liquid. He touched the tip of his finger to his tongue.

Immediately, the taste of an herbal tea with all chemical compounds flowed through his brain. He stood and quickly searched the rooms. He returned to the area. His eyes glowed as he changed his field of vision. Near the replicator was the footprint of one of the males.

Jar scanned the handle of the cleansing unit, documenting the fingerprints on the handle to the processor in his brain. His mind scanned the crew documents and discovered the man had just transferred over from the disabled warship an hour before they departed Elpidios.

Jar carefully opened the cleansing unit and discovered a cracked cup sitting on the top shelf. His mind processed the information in rapid order and he drew a conclusion that sent an unusual shiver of emotion through him. He tapped into the warship's computer system again and did a ship wide scan for the little female. Deck after deck, department after department came up with a negative.

He finally sent a command to retrieve her last known location. Within seconds, the disposal bay responded. He sent one more request, even as he dreaded the response he knew he would get.

"Crew member Star Strauss, ejected from liquid waste port three," the computer responded.

Jar linked into Jazin's comlink even as he was locating the video recording of the corridor and the location of the crew members whose prints he had on file. The man was in the shuttle bay. Jar opened communication's with Dakar and Armet at the same time as Jazin answered.

"Is she safe?" Jazin asked tensely.

"Dakar, apprehend crewman Delant. He is needed for questioning. Expect deadly resistance. Armet, get to the disposal bay and check the system for the last disposal location. Jazin, your female was ejected from the *Blue Star*," Jar responded coldly. "I wish permission to interrogate Ensign Delant for his role in her abduction," Jar paused as he received the video feed. His eyes flickered brightly as the information poured in. He fast forwarded until he received the information he wanted. "I will also need Ensign Corklar."

"I will get Corklar," Armet snarled. "I just passed him heading for engineering."

Jazin stood frozen as he listened to Jarmen. All his mind could process was Star had been ejected from the ship into open space. He gripped the railing as his knees threatened to give out on him. He closed his eyes and pulled her beautiful face into his mind. A cold, deadly rage built. He would get the information that he needed from the traitors, one slice at a time.

* * *

Star groaned as she came to. Her head throbbed like someone was beating on a bass drum for the first time in music class. One thing was for sure, they were having one hell of a party by the feel of it. She hoped drummer was enjoying it because she sure as hell wasn't!

She opened her eyes and felt a moment of uncontrollable terror. She opened her mouth to scream, but all that came out was a tiny whimper. Star raised her hands as far as she could and felt along the side of the container she was trapped in.

Her mind played every horror movie she had ever seen where someone was buried alive. She was definitely in some type of container. Her breathing accelerated as a full fledge panic attack threatened to overwhelm her.

"Respiration has increased," a calm voice stated. "Reduce breathing by using deep breaths to calm your intake."

"Where…. Where am I?" Star whispered hoarsely.

"Relax and continue to breathe as normally as possible. Escape pod guidelines provide for the minimum oxygen levels to extend the possibility of rescue. Passengers who do not panic can extend levels by two additional hours if they remain calm. Rescue beacon is active and has been answered. Retrieval in approximately twenty-four minutes, eight seconds."

The voice continued to repeat the instructions every few minutes until Star felt like screaming just to get it to shut up. She got the message already. She was stuck, someone was on their way, breathe slowly.

Star remained still, looking up at the dimly lit interior. Taking a deep breath, she focused on what she could remember and tried to fill in the blanks. The two men had obviously been responsible for her being here.

The million dollar question was why did they do it and what did they want. If Star had to guess, she would place all of the chips on Tai Tek being behind her abduction. That guy was really beginning to piss her off. She bet he was behind all the other sudden 'situations' as well. That guy either had way too much charisma which she obviously wasn't seeing or he had money, or credits in this case, coming out the yin-yang.

Star flexed her fingers in the soft cloth interior and frowned when the tips of her fingers brushed something small and hard. She wiggled further down and searched along the crevice with her fingers until she felt it again. She rolled it between her fingers. A soft sob escaped her as she recognized the comlink she had been reaching for before the jerk stunned her. She wasn't sure how far it would work, but it was a chance of rescue, no matter how slim.

She felt around it until she found the tiny button on the side. She drew in another deep breath and pressed the button. It was linked directly to Jazin's, no one else, just his.

"Jazin," Star called out loudly. "Jazin, please you have to hear me."

"Star," Jazin's voice came over the comlink. It was weak, but it was his voice. Static made it impossible to hear what he was saying so she didn't even try.

"Jazin, I'm in some kind of a box. You have to help me. The computer said something was coming," Star sobbed. "Please, you have to hear me. Jazin, I'm in a box. It feels like a coffin. I don't like coffins."

The box jerked and a loud bang sounded on the outside of it near Star's head. "Retrieval in progress. Life support is stable. Congratulations passenger, you are safe," the automated voice said before the lights in the box turned off plunging Star into darkness.

"Jazin, they have me," Star whispered brokenly.

..*

Jazin's harsh cry of fury echoed through the level. The sound so loud and painful that the warriors in the area, paused for a moment and bowed their head. The moment Star's voice activated his comlink, Jar had boosted the reception. He could do it coming in, but not going out.

The sound of his mate's tortured voice tore through Jazin's tightly held control. He gripped the laser sword he had retrieved from his living quarters. The two crewmen had been taken to the training room. He had ordered it cleared of everything. When he got done with the men, the room would be coated in their blood.

The men were on their knees, their arms secured behind their backs when he walked in. Both men glared defiantly up at Jazin as he walked through the door. Their glares turned to fear as they studied his face. Jazin stared at each man before he nodded to Armet and Dakar to pull them up into a standing position.

"You might as well kill us," the taller man, Corklar, stated coldly. "You will get nothing out of us."

Jazin's smile turned the men's blood to ice. He took a step closer, appraising each man carefully. He raised his hand and gripped Delant's throat, squeezing slowly until he began to gag. Jazin grimly shook his head.

"You will not die so easily," he whispered in a dark, menacing tone devoid of emotion. "I am going to slice you up one small piece at a time. You will beg for death and I will still deny you the comfort of it. You will learn the penalty of harming the mate of a Kassisan Lord. We are unbelievable cruel when someone harms what belongs to us."

The door behind him opened and two men entered with a small cart. Both men turned white when they saw the medical cart. Their eyes swung back to Jazin. Delant's throat worked up and down frantically.

"Jar," Jazin called out quietly. Jar stepped forward and removed the hood from the cloak that he always wore. "I want everything."

Jar turned his glowing amber eyes to Delant. "I will discover everything, my friend, everything."

Delant's screams filled the room as Jar laid the tips of his fingers on the male's temple. Thin fibers burst through the tips of them, drilling through bone, and into the soft tissue of the man's brain. Jarmen accessed the male's memory. His eyes burned brightly as he downloaded the images. Every memory the man had now belonged to Jarmen.

The process was not painful for Jarmen, but it could be for the recipient of the probe. Jarmen had the capacity to block the pain if he chose, but he didn't. When he finished with Delant, the male would have sunk down to the floor limply if Dakar would have let him.

Jarmen smiled at Corklar blandly. "Next," he said calmly.

"No," Corklar shouted hoarsely. "No, I'll tell you everything you want to know. I swear, I'll tell you everything."

Jazin nodded to Jarmen to continue. "Yes, you will," Jar said as he touched his fingers to Corklar's temples. "You will tell us everything."

Chapter 18

Star slipped the comlink into the pocket of her pants as she felt the box she was in being roughly handled. She closed her eyes and focused on her breathing. This was just like when she helped Marcus the Magnificent, the most famous magician in all the world when he needed an assistant.

Marcus was really Marcus Jones, a pickpocket from Vegas that learned the tricks of the trade on the streets before Walter caught him sneaking into the circus when he was twenty. His name changed and so did his life. Marcus had taught Star, Jo, and River how to pick every lock that was ever made.

He said you never knew when you might find yourself trapped in a five hundred year old dungeon or in a thirty year old jail cell. He had also been thrown into a few trunks by local drug dealers and pimps determined to give him a new home under the brilliant Nevada skies.

In fact, many of the circus performers had skills they learned on the streets or, as in the case of Bombing Bill, in the military. He perfected his skills when he got out by doing special effects for Hollywood before he came to a show one night. He had fallen in love with the magic and beauty of the performers. Walter found him sitting on the steps of his trailer the next morning with nothing more than a sad look and a battered suitcase.

Star let her memories calm her as the box was set down. She refused to leave the world she remembered as she needed to remain as calm as possible until an opportunity presented itself. The lid of the container slid backwards slowly. Musky air circulated around her and she had to fight not to sneeze from it. The instant the lid was clear, Star erupted upwards.

She struck out like Armet and Dakar taught her with a little bit of Walter thrown in for good measure. Her feet connected with one man's nose while her palm caught the one bending over her in the throat. She rolled up, doing a handstand before flipping out of the container. She looked at the two men. Both were on their knees. The one she kicked in the nose was groaning as blood flowed down his face. The one she hit in the throat was gagging.

Star didn't wait. She moved forward, grabbing the one gagging by the back of his head and slamming him face first into the metal box as hard as she could. The second man tried to roll to his feet and grab for the pistol attached to his side. Star kicked out again, feeling an immense sense of satisfaction at the sound of bone crushing under her booted foot.

It was amazing how strong you could be when you are scared shitless, she thought to herself as she pulled the pistol tucked in the man's waistband out and shot both of them at close range.

She looked down at the settings when she didn't see any blood and breathed a sigh of relief that it was set to stun. She looked around, swinging the pistol up and pointing it in case anyone else came along. It looked like she was in some type of small freighter.

She listened carefully, but she didn't hear anything but her own heavy breathing.

"Okay, now I need help moving your asses somewhere where you can't wake up and get me," Star muttered as she stared down at the two unconscious figures.

She turned with a squeak and pointed the pistol as another figure came forward. "You requested assistance?" The metal figure asked with a twitch to its head.

"Y… Yes, I do. What are you?" Star asked hesitantly.

"I am Numbnuts, a class A service bot," the metal figure responded.

"They named you Numbnuts?" Star choked out on a startled giggle. "For real?"

"Yes, I am real. You requested assistance," Numbnuts responded with another twitch.

"Can you help me secure these two so they can't get loose? I don't want them to hurt me. What I really need is a way to lock them up and take control of this…. Whatever it is," Star said, looking around the dingy freighter.

"This is a First Class Piece of Shit," Numbnuts stated as he bent over and gripped the back of each man's shirt. "I will secure them in the shithole."

Star giggled as Numbnuts turned and began dragging the two men she had knocked out down along the long, metal corridor. She couldn't help but wince and feel a little sorry for the two. Their asses were going to be raw by the time the service bot got them to the 'shithole'.

Numbnuts dropped both men in the middle of the corridor. Star watched in fascination as the service bot bent over and pulled up a section of the floor, it was hollow underneath the panel. Thick metal bars covered the hole that was about the size of the dumpsters back home.

Numbnuts lifted the metal hatch and slid it to the side. At the bottom of the hole was what looked like a port-a-potty. There were also several piles of blankets and a lot of empty bottles. Numbnuts picked up one of the bodies and dropped the man on the pile of blankets where he promptly rolled off onto the cold, metal floor. He turned and did the same thing to the next man. Once he was done, he slid the metal bars back over the top and slid a locking device into place.

"Do you wish to cover the Shithole or not?" Numbnuts asked Star who was watching the whole process with wide-eyed amazement.

"What do you normally do?" Star asked, biting her lower lip.

"It depends. If Dumbass is drunk and annoying then Jackoff requests that I do. If Jackoff is drunk and annoying then I do not. Dumbass says it is easier for him to throw things at him without the covering."

"Are you telling me those two use this on each other?" Star asked faintly.

"Yes," Numbnuts responded. "Unless they are being boarded by an Alliance ship. Then they hide their illegal cargo in the shithole."

"What kind of illegal cargo?" Star asked curiously.

"They specialize in the trafficking of a foul liquid that often causes them to become quite loud and annoying," Numbnuts said waiting to see if he should cover them or not.

Star glanced down at the two men who were snoring loudly now. She giggled when one of them rolled over and snuggled the other. Something told her these were not the typical warriors Tai Tek normally hired.

"Don't cover them up and whatever you do, don't let them get out!" Star ordered. "Is there anyone else on this piece of shit?"

"Only IQ," Numbnuts answered, tossing the cover plating to one side of the corridor.

"And who is IQ?" Star asked, wondering if whatever it was could be any more wacky.

"IQ. You call IQ? What now, Numbnuts? I'm busy. Someone has to work on this piece of shit," a very small robot about a foot and a half tall rolled up in a ball and uncurled until it was standing on two legs with wheels attached to the ends.

"Oh," Star gasped. "Hello."

IQ turned on his wheels and scanned Star. "Ah, my beautiful little butterfly. Have you come just for me?" He purred rolling up to her. "I'm IQ. I will bring your every fantasy to life," the tiny robot murmured in a voice that reminded Star of Pepé Le Pew, the adorable skunk from the cartoon show.

The tiny robot reached out an arm, or at least she thought it was an arm, and grasped her hand firmly between its three digits. The head leaned over and the creature pressed his mouth to the back of her hand before turning it over and doing the same to her palm. Star jerked her hand back when she felt something slimy touch it. She glanced down and saw a faint line of oil along her palm. Gross!

"Oh my beautiful darling, I will make your life amazing," IQ purred as he rolled up to her leg and began feeling her up.

"IQ is the pilot. He has been trying to teach Dumbass and Jackoff how to navigate the ship, but they are not very fast learners. They won this ship in a game of chance two years ago and still have not mastered the controls. IQ and I were already part of the crew."

Star looked down at the tiny creature looking up at her with two mismatched eyes that blinked slowly at different times. *Okay, this is getting way too weird for me,* she thought with a giggle. She was used to a lot of strange things in her life, but this had to be the absolute strangest.

"IQ, can you contact someone for me?" Star asked politely trying to move her leg away. If she wasn't mistaken, she would swear the tiny robot was trying to hump it.

"Of course, my love. IQ will do anything for you," the tiny robot responded before turning on his wheels and heading along the corridor at a rapid clip.

* * *

"Send in a cleaning crew and jettison the bodies," Jazin said, ignoring the looks he received as he walked down the corridor.

He was covered in blood. None of it was his. He had been ruthless, cold, deadly. He showed no mercy. Dakar, Armet, and Jarmen had stood to the side never interfering and never condemning his brutality against the men who struck out against his family, especially his mate. He wanted to set an example of what would happen to anyone who dared.

The training room was a blood bath. He looked almost as bad. Blood covered him from head to foot. His chest was bare, long streaks of blood mixed with sweat ran down in eerie trails.

Dakar, Jarmen, and Armet followed behind him. Blood splatters covered the three of them, evidence of the violence behind the punishment. The sight of the young lord struck terror into those who saw him as he approached the bridge.

During the three hours it took for him to kill the two men, the emergency teams had repaired most of the damage to the warship and taken in the Tearnat warriors before their ship imploded. Jarmen informed him the warship's engines would be back online within the next hour.

The men paused as he approached, bowing their heads in respect. Even the Tearnat warriors kneeled and placed their palms over their hearts in a show of respect and loyalty. Jazin walked onto the bridge without saying a word. He looked briefly at Jarmen who nodded. His friend closed his eyes and focused.

When he opened them, his eyes blazed with power as he tapped into the communications system and opened it to every Kassisan, Elpidios, Tearnat, and Alliance ship within receiving distance.

"My name is Jazin Ja Kel Coradon. I am the third son of the ruling House of Kassis. Let it be known that any who strike against my family or my mate will be given no mercy. Death will not come fast enough. For the ones who have taken my mate, there is no place you can hide that I will not find you, no star system that can protect you, and no Gods that will give you mercy. I am coming for my mate and I am bringing death with me," he growled out in an icy voice.

Jarmen closed his eyes, releasing the communications console back to the warrior in charge of it. Slowly, one by one, the warriors on the bridge rose. The men looked proudly at Jazin's bloody figure before kneeling.

Each man bowed his head and placed a clenched fist against their heart. Jazin could have traveled throughout the great warship and found the same thing. Tearnat and Kassisan warriors knelt together in unity. There are many things that a true warrior holds scared, his mate being the most important.

Jazin's jaw clenched. He would not show what the loss of Star was doing to him. He turned, nodding to Armet and Dakar. He looked at Jarmen who nodded in response to his silent order to follow him. As the door opened, a soft voice echoed through the warship's communication system.

"Were you able to connect?" Star's anxious voice sounded.

"Of course, my love. You have sound but no video, I'm afraid. I wish I could do more," the deep masculine voice purred. "I would connect the universe to bring a smile to your face."

Jazin turned in disbelief as his mate's giggle echoed through the bridge. "You don't have to do that, you adorable bundle of sweetness. I just need to talk with a warship called the *Blue Star*."

"All they need to hear is the sweet sound of your voice, my gorgeous oil can, and they would search for the beautiful face that goes with it," the male said smoothly.

"Connect the transmission to a secure line on the commander's console," Jazin growled out turning to look briefly at Jarmen.

Jarmen nodded before closing his eyes and redirecting the transmission as Jazin requested. "It is done."

Jazin stormed into the conference room, pacing back and forth while he drew in deep breaths to calm himself. Jarmen came in behind him and sealed the door. Jazin looked at his friend with such fury, Jarmen winced. He had just killed two men. He had also opened communications to every known star system with a vow of vengeance and now his mate calls him giggling! Giggling! Jazin ran his blood stained hands through his hair and fought the need to scream in fury. He was going to rip apart the male who continued to whisper sweet nothings to his mate.

"Where in the Gods are you, Star? And who is the male?" Jazin growled out stopping long enough to grip the chair that was bolted to the floor.

"Jazin? Oh Jazin, I was so scared. I don't know where I am? IQ honey, do you know where we are?" Star asked softly.

"Of course, my dream. We are in space."

Star giggled again. "Oh Jazin! Do you get it? I asked him where we were and he said we were in space! Isn't he the cutest thing you've ever heard? He calls me all these ridiculous names, but he really is smart and such a sweetheart," Star added.

"Star, I need to know what your location is?" Jazin said in a quiet voice that reflected none of the violence he was feeling at the moment.

"Oh, yeah, sorry."

Jazin listened as Star cleared her throat and asked the male what their location was again. This time, the male gave him the needed coordinates. Once he had them, he programmed the information into the warship's navigation system. Now, he just needed to know who had his mate so he could kill them.

"Star, how were you able to contact the *Blue Star*?" Jazin asked, rocking back and forth as his fingers flexed in a crushing grip on the chair back.

"Oh, the box I was in was pulled aboard a freighter called *Piece of Shit*. When the two men on board opened it, I used the defense moves Armet and Dakar taught me to take them down. Jazin, you should have seen me! I kicked their asses good. Oh, you won't believe their names! One of the men is called Dumbass and the other is called Jackoff. Anyway, I was able to get a pistol one of the guys was wearing and I shot them, only it was set to stun so I didn't really hurt them, but it knocked them out good," Star paused to draw in a breath.

Jazin leaned his forehead down on the chair as he listened to her excited tone. She didn't sound the least bit afraid now. His head jerked up as he realized she said she had stunned the men, not killed them. Gods, that meant they could still hurt her.

"Star, what about the men?" Jazin asked anxiously.

"Oh, you don't have to worry about them. Numbnuts, that's the service bot, has them locked up in the shithole," she said mildly. "So, that only leaves me, IQ, and Numbnuts manning this piece of shit," Star finished before she burst into laughter. "This is so good, Jazin. There is no way I could ever have made this 'shit' up," she added before she burst into laughter that bordered on hysteria.

Jazin's heart twisted when he heard the catch in her voice as she finally calmed down. "Jazin, can you come get me?"

"I will be there in less than an hour," he responded huskily. "And I want time alone with the crew."

Star giggled as IQ began singing a love song in French of all languages. "I think it might be an interesting conversation."

"Keep the line open at all times," Jazin gritted over the noise of the singing. "I don't want to lose our connection."

"I will. Oh, I think Dumbass and Jackoff are waking up," Star said breathlessly. "I'd better go have a talk with them."

"Star," Jazin growled out but all he could hear was that damn male voice singing in some language he didn't understand and that didn't translate. "STAR!" He barked out loudly.

"I will monitor communications," Jarmen said coming up behind his friend. "Perhaps it would be best for you to get cleaned up. Your mate should not see you covered in blood the way you are."

Jazin looked down at his hands. Jar was right. With a muttered curse, he turned toward the door. As it opened, he looked back at his friend and pointed to the communication's console.

"I am going to kill that annoying bastard," he growled out before he turned and the door closed behind him.

Jarmen winced as the male on the other end hit a particularly high note and held it for a long time. "I will help you, my friend, I will gladly help you."

Chapter 19

Star gripped the pistol she had tightly between both her palms as she edged up to the hole in the floor. She could hear muted conversation as the men talked to each other. She paused, listening for a few minutes. Shaking her head, she frowned in confusion. The men were speaking in French! One man was trying to tell the other that he still loved him, black eyes and all. The other man moaned that his nose would make him uglier now.

"Luc, I would love you no matter how crooked your nose was," the one man assured him in a deeply accented voice.

"We weren't supposed to open the box, Jon Paul," Luc replied. "The man said that we were only to pick up a box in space, do not open it, and he would buy this piece of shit from us when we delivered it still sealed to him! How are we going to open a restaurant now?"

"You will just have to win one in a poker game for us," Jon Paul responded lightly.

"Bonjour messieurs," Star called down in a soft, hesitant voice. "Mon nom est Star Strauss. Avec qui dois-je le plaisir de parler?" She asked in French.

Both men looked up, startled. The man she had hit in the throat stood up and bowed his head in greeting. "Bonjour Madame. I am Jon Paul and this is my partner, Luc. We are your humble servants from the most romantic city on a planet called Earth."

"Paris?" Star giggled with a raised eyebrow.

"Aucun," Jon Paul answered with a wicked smile. "Montreal, Canada."

"So how did two French Canadians end up owning a piece of shit freighter in the middle of a distant star system?" Star asked switching to English as she sat down cross-legged near the opening.

"It is a long, but magnificent story of true love, pirates, and a wonderful game of chance," Jon Paul said with a mischievous grin. "Would you like to hear our amazing story of adventure?"

"Yes," Star giggled. "I think I would."

Luc slowly stood up and gave Star a pained smile. "And you will share your story of how you ended up in Snow White's magical box, as well, oui? The stories would go much better with a bottle of wine," he added in a slightly hopeful voice. "As well as help with the pain to both my nose and my pride that such a tiny, beautiful fairy could take down two such big, but lovable Frenchmen."

Star laughed out loud. "I'll let you out, but be warned, if you try to hurt me my boyfriend is going to be very, very upset with you," she teased as she stood up. "By the way, did you really name your service bot Numbnuts?" She whispered.

Luc's face twisted again as Jon Paul burst into laughter. "That my lovely fairy, is yet another story."

* * *

By the time the *Blue Star* arrived, Star had fallen in love with the two adorable Frenchmen who had emigrated from Paris to Montreal to start their own restaurant. The men told her how they had been returning from a farm that was renowned for its cheeses when the SUV they were driving got a flat tire. The two had been arguing so much about the proper way to change a tire they didn't notice the strange lights in the sky until it was too late. They woke on a strange spaceship.

The group of pirates who planned to sell them decided to keep the men after Jon Paul and Luc convinced the captain to let them cook for the crew. They had spent the next ten years cooking and fighting alongside the mismatched group of misfits that made up the pirate crew.

Two years ago, the captain decided she wanted to retire. The ship was sold and Jon Paul and Luc found themselves on a distant Spaceport with a few credits and the little knowledge they had learned during their years aboard the pirate ship. Luc was a master at poker and he introduced the game at the bar on the Spaceport. It became a huge success and the bar owner let the two men stay on for about six months with the promise of a place to stay and all the liquor they wanted in exchange for holding poker games.

One night, a horrid man came in. Fascinated with the game, he played and played until all he had left to chance was the *Dread*, the short haul freighter that was two trips shy of the scrap pile. Luc won the freighter in the card game. The next morning, he and Jon Paul woke up with a massive hangover in the middle of space in what they called a 'piece of shit'. The name stuck.

The only thing they were truly grateful for was it came with IQ and Numbnuts, neither the original name of the service bots. Since neither Luc or Jon Paul knew the first thing about piloting a spaceship they relied on the service bots to pilot it. Both service bots received some slight reprogramming over the last two years which is why they acted the way they did. Jon Paul and Luc's new names had come about the evening they first woke up. They had traded insults with each other for having found themselves in yet another strange mess. The service bots had picked it up and it stuck since neither man could figure out how to un-program the names from the bots' memory.

"We have guests, Dumbass. They have boarded without permission," IQ said over the communication's console attached to the wall. "Should I tell them to blow off or are they expected."

"First, we need to know if they are friends or enemies. How else do we know whether to offer them a glass of wine or not?" Jon Paul replied with a grin.

"You will know exactly what I am when I cut you both into small pieces," Jazin snarled out, stepping through the narrow opening leading into the small kitchen area.

"Jazin!" Star squealed, jumping up from her seat and throwing herself into his arms. "You came!"

Jazin retracted his laser sword as Star threw her tiny body into his and began pressing kisses to his face. His arms tightened around her and he pulled her close, inhaling her sweet fragrance. The feel of her, safe and secure, against him sent waves of relief coursing through his body. Jazin had Jar monitor the communications as best he could, but the male called IQ had been no help. The damn male had driven Jar nuts with his singing, constant questions about what he looked like, and innuendos as he tried to find out if Jar was into open relationships.

"What do you mean, I came? Of course I would come," Jazin said huskily.

His eyes moved to focus on the two males sitting across the small table staring at them. They had their arms around each other and watched him as if they were old friends. One of the male's actually had his head on the other's shoulder. Both were smiling at him with a goofy grin, not the terror they should have been.

"Ah, amour," Luc sighed in contentment. "Do they not make a beautiful couple, Jon Paul?"

Star giggled softly and leaned up to whisper in Jazin's ear. "The one with the black eyes is Luc. The other is Jon Paul. They are from my planet and they are very much in love with each other."

Jazin pulled back and stared down at Star in surprise before he looked back at both men in sudden understanding. "So who is the other male that was talking to you?" Jazin growled out looking around. He wanted to kill someone, maybe not the two men grinning at him like fools, but someone.

"That was IQ," Star said with a huge smile. "He's the pilot."

"You called, my love?"

The husky male voice that had been driving Jar up the wall for the past hour called out. Jazin and Jar turned at the same time, raising their swords. Both men stopped, their mouths hanging open, as the tiny service bot rolled up and uncurled at their feet.

"Well hello good-looking!" IQ said looking up into Jar's glowing amber eyes. "You can play with my programming anytime." A low, sexy purr rumbled from the tiny bot.

"Gentlemen, please meet IQ. The pilot of this piece of shit," Star said right before she burst into laughter. "Oh Jazin, I can't wait to tell Jo and River about this!"

Jarmen growled down at the little service bot that had moved forward and was running one of its arms up his leg while saying things he did not understand. He shook it off with a grunt of disgust and shot a frigid glare at the two men who chuckled in delight. They might think it was funny but he did not. He closed his eyes and focused on the tiny bot. In seconds, he had reprogrammed it back to its original status with a few minor improvements.

Let's see if they like this! Jar thought as he opened his eyes again. The little bot rocked back and forth before just standing silent with a frozen look on its metallic face.

"Jar!" Star cried out in disappointment. "I liked him the way he was. You program him back to the way he was right this instant!"

Jar turned and looked at the pouting face of the tiny warrior that was wrapped tightly around his friend and sighed deeply. His friend wasn't the only one she had wrapped around her tiny fingers. His eyes glowed again before he looked down at her with a frown.

"If he starts humping my leg again, I'll overheat his circuit boards," he growled out before pointing at the two men who burst out laughing at him. "That goes for both of you as well."

Luc picked up the bottle of homemade wine off the table and took a huge swallow of it before he wiped his hand across the back of his mouth and replied. "My glow-friend, the tiny fairy has already beaten you to it! Can you not see my eyes and nose? Is she not magnificent?"

Jazin growled softly as the men went on and on about what the beautiful fairy did to them and how enchanted they were with her. He was more than ready to return to the *Blue Star* when the old freighter shuddered and groaned, knocking them sideways.

He and Jarmen had come in using a small, service shuttle so they could not be detected. It was currently docked to the service hatch under the freighter. The shuttle was just big enough for two people. Their plan was to board the freighter, secure Star somewhere safe, and kill the men who took her. Armet and Dakar were on their way with the Tearnat Starship. The *Blue Star* would meet up with them once it was back online and would destroy the freighter after they were safely back aboard the warship. Now, it looked like someone else had the same thought.

"Dumbass, someone is hailing us! The dippy wad who wants to buy our home. What should I tell him?"

IQ called out through the communications console in the wall.

"What do we tell him?" Jon Paul asked as the freighter rocked again. "Numbnuts! Get in here! Do you know if we have shields? Guns? Anything?"

Jazin and Jarmen looked at both men as they huddled next to each other. "You two don't even know if you have any defense systems on board?" Jazin asked in disbelief.

"We French are lovers, not fighters. The only weapon we had your beautiful fairy took from us," Luc said with an apologetic smile.

"That is not true!" Jon Paul said fiercely. "The French are some of the greatest fighters in history! We are known for our skills in battle."

"Oui, that is true. There was the French Revolution, World War I and II, not to mention the French Foreign Legion," Luc started to say with a weak smile. "But, me? I am definitely more of a lover."

"The French Foreign Legion is made up of many nationalities, isn't it?" Star asked as she clung to Jazin who was braced against the table.

"Can we discuss this later?" Jazin bit out. "Jarmen, tap into their system and see if there is anything you can do to keep us from being blown apart. You," Jazin said, pointing to Jon Paul. "You will make contact and find out what is going on. Tell him you have what he wants and try to get him to board."

"What about me?" Luc said as Jon Paul scooted out from behind the table and headed for the bridge. "What should I do?"

Jazin fought the urge to tell the man what he really wanted to tell him. The first suggestion was for the strange human to take an escape pod so it could be used as target practice instead of the freighter. Instead, he told the man to secure any items that might cause damage to the freighter, hoping that would keep him busy for a while. The man left, followed closely by the tall service bot.

"The freighter's shields are holding at seventy percent," Jarmen said looking at Jazin. "There are two laser gun ports mounted. One on top, the other is down below. No power to either one so they are useless."

Jazin nodded even as he listened to the sound of voices coming from the front. "Can you monitor the conversation from here?"

"Of course," Jarmen said, tilting his head to the side and enhancing his hearing. "It is Tai Tek. He picked up the distress signal that little warrior sent out. The one named Jon Paul is telling him that they opened the box and found a human female," Jar's mouth tilted up at the corner. "The human male is cursing Tai Tek out in a combination of languages. I am not able to completely translate what he is saying, but I think it's safe to say he is calling Tai Tek a cowardly bastard and challenging him to a duel."

"What the hell is a duel?" Jazin asked in exasperation. He didn't think this situation could get any worse.

"A duel is when a man defends his honor by challenging someone who has insulted it to fight, usually to the death," Star said as she gripped Jazin's arm tightly. "You aren't going to let him fight Tai Tek, are you? I don't want Jon Paul to get hurt."

Jazin gritted his teeth as he stared down into the worried eyes of his mate. This is why he wanted to lock her up. She was far too tender-hearted! He couldn't help but wonder which God or Goddess he had insulted in his previous lives. Only his mate could get kidnapped, ejected into space, and end up on a dilapidated freighter with no weapons systems and a crew of four, two of whom were totally clueless to any type of survival skills. The only two who could probably fight were the service bots!

A curse burst from his lips as the freighter rocked again. "Armet! Where in the hell are you?" Jazin barked out. "Dakar, how long until the *Blue Star's* engines are back online?"

"Ten minutes out," Armet answered tightly.

"They are coming online now," Dakar responded. "The *Blue Star* can be there in twenty minutes."

"We may not have ten minutes much less twenty," Jazin bit out. "This rusted pile of scrap has no defense systems."

"Gods!" Armet cursed. "I'm pushing the starship. I can cut a few extra minutes off."

Jazin could hear Dakar ordering engineering to get the *Blue Star* up to full power immediately. He looked down at Star. She was staring at him with total trust in her eyes. His heart thudded heavily. She was magnificent.

"I love you, my Star," he said huskily. "Now, sit your ass down until we can get out of here."

"Jazin, they are sending a boarding party," Jarmen warned. "Expect company, they are attaching to the emergency hatch now."

"We have an emergency hatch?" Luc asked as he hurried back into the small kitchen area.

Jazin just shook his head and nodded to Jarmen. "You will stay here and protect my mate with your life," he growled out.

"Oui, oui, with my life," Luc said as Jon Paul and IQ came down from the bridge.

Jazin took one more look at the man with his two black eyes and his broken nose and groaned. "Go!" He snapped out to Jarmen.

* * *

Tai Tek yelled out orders to the Commander of the Tearnat warship he was on. They only had minutes before they would need to disappear. The commander warned him that a Kassian warship was less than fifteen minutes out.

He had ordered the group of mercenaries to kill the human males and capture the female. He needed the female. It was obvious from the young Kassian lord's resistance when he had been held at the fortress that the male would not break. He needed the technology the young lord had on the defense systems.

He was running out of resources and the technology would not only give him the tools he needed to defeat the House of Kassis but he could also sell some of it to help finance his rebellion since the middle lord, Manota, had found some of his hidden accounts and seized the credits in them. He was growing desperate and desperate men did what was necessary to win.

Besides, he owed the little white haired warrior. The knife the dark haired female threw ended up in his shoulder, but the little warrior's crossbow had not missed either. He thought of the body it had struck. His lover had been standing next to him. The only thing he cared about beyond the power of ruling Kassis.

It had been his plan to have his bodyguard and lover by his side when he ruled. Now, Narus was dead. Fury and the need for revenge burned through him as he thought of the male who had stood beside him since they were children. He wanted to kill the female slowly so she could feel his pain and he wanted the young lord to see and hear her as he did.

"Tell your men they have two minutes to grab the female," Tai Tek snapped out.

"Sir, they are encountering resistance," the commander responded.

Tai Tek turned to the commander in fury. "How can two weak human males with no weapons resist ten of your mercenaries?" He asked coldly.

The commander of the Tearnat warship turned with a stony face. "That is how."

Tai Tek turned as a familiar voice came over the communication's console. "Tai Tek, you are a dead man," Jazin said coldly. "The men you sent are dead and you will be joining them shortly. You will never touch my mate."

Tai Tek stepped back as the icy voice washed over him. A shiver of dread racked his body briefly as he listened to the deep promise in the words. He motioned for the commander to get them out of there even as the ship rocked from a blast to its shields. He cursed silently at having been defeated again.

"I am not dead yet, Lord Jazin," Tai Tek responded furiously. "You cannot keep her safe forever. When you least expect it, I will be there to warm your spot by her side."

"Not in this lifetime, you miserable prick!" Star called out. "You want a piece of me, you little twerp, bring it on!"

Tai Tek cut communications to the freighter and turned to the commander of the Tearnat ship Trolis had given him. "Open fire on the freighter then get us out of here!" Tai Tek snapped to the commander. "I should have known he wouldn't be so brave if he did not have re-enforcements close by," he snarled as another blast rocked the warship.

"What about my men?" The commander asked.

"They are already dead," Tai Tek said, turning and leaving the bridge.

* * *

Jazin grabbed Star around the waist with one arm and placed his hand over her mouth with the other. Her muffled curses and threats could still be heard. He let go of her mouth when she swung her arm around almost clobbering him in the head. His hand gripped her wrist and he looked pointedly at the pan she held in her hand.

"Luc wouldn't give me the laser pistol," she muttered. "He said he needed it to protect me if the bad guys got past you and Jarmen and made it into the kitchen."

"Where is he now?" Jazin asked.

"Jon Paul is with him," she said, turning in his arms and dropping the pan to the floor where it bounced with a loud clatter against the metal floor. "I was so scared," she whispered before she pulled his lips down to hers in a desperate kiss fueled by fear and relief.

Jar came onto the bridge followed by IQ. Jazin looked up in warning even as he deepened the kiss. He could feel his brave little warrior's body shaking as she pressed up against him. The fight had been short, but fierce. There had been ten men. They had cut them down as they entered the storage bay.

Things had gotten hairy when one of the men tried to blow the hatch they had entered through. The storage bay had decompressed, shutting the automatic seals. Both he and Jar would have been swept out into space if not for the large service bot. It had grabbed both of them by their arms, activated the magnetic grips on its feet and pulled them out while

Jar held the door open just long enough for them to get through.

Jazin pulled back with a sigh as alarms began sounding as the blast from the Tearnat warship burst through the shields. "We are all going to die!" IQ wailed as he came rolling up to Jarmen.

"We are not going to die," Jazin said in exasperation. "Jar, how long do we have?"

"A minute, maybe two," Jar responded. "If we don't find a way off this thing, we are all going to die."

Star tiredly rested her head against Jazin's chest. "What next?"

Jon Paul and Luc came scrambling into the bridge carrying a large box between them that clanked and clattered as glass knocked against each other. Both men had a huge grin on their face. Jazin looked at the ceiling briefly before he looked back at Jar in resignation.

"We are packed and ready to go," Luc said excitedly.

"Armet, where are you? We could use a way off this thing before it explodes," Jazin said, moving toward the service hatch they had entered.

"I'm docking under the freighter now. I hope you weren't attached to that maintenance shuttle," Armet said calmly. "You better put a move on. This bucket of bolts doesn't look too good."

Chapter 20

They had escaped the freighter with not a second to spare. Jon Paul and Luc had toasted their goodbye to the freighter cheerfully while IQ kept trying to snuggle up to Jarmen. Jar had finally shut the little service bot down.

Star didn't know if it was because he was embarrassed or so he could get some peace and quiet. Numbnuts had promptly requested permission to recharge and shut down on his own. By the time they were safely back on board the *Blue Star*, Tai Tek had pulled another disappearing act. She knew that all the men were frustrated, but they also felt more confident than ever that it was just a matter of time before he was caught.

Jazin told Star that Manota and Jo had returned along with Star's parents and a wide assortment of other characters. He didn't tell her that Manota swore that half of their new passengers must have been from a dozen or more bizarre different species! His normally quiet brother looked extremely agitated.

"What is wrong?" Jazin had asked once Dakar, Armet, and Jarmen had left to get some much needed rest. "Did you encounter problems returning to our mates' world?"

"Yes," Manota admitted reluctantly. "We had to bring a few additional passengers that were not a part of Jo and Star's family or the circus. There were two members of their world's security force that followed us. I was left with no choice but to bring them with us."

"Who else?" Jazin asked concerned.

"The one called Walter found a young female who had been beaten the night we were to leave. She needed immediate medical care," Manota said quietly. "I had no choice but to bring her with us. I am not sure if she will heal, at least mentally. She still had not spoken. Jo, her parents, and a few of the others spend time with her."

Jazin felt a wave of unease. "How did our mates' parents react to you?" He asked hesitantly.

"Jazin, these creatures….," Manota drew in a deep breath before he looked over his shoulder to make sure he was alone. "They are some of the most unusual I have ever seen."

"What happened?" Jazin asked bluntly.

He wanted to get back to his mate. He didn't have time to try to decipher what Manota was reluctant to share. He was too damn tired anyway. Personally, he could care less if Star's parents accepted him. She was his and he would never let her go. He leaned forward, rubbing his brow tiredly, and looked at his brother. He had never seen him look so uncertain before.

"Tell me," Jazin said impatiently.

"Her parents were so happy to see Jo and know that their daughters were safe, they did not question who I was at first. Of course, that changed after they discovered where I planned to take her and them. The next thing I knew, I have a hundred different beings, supposedly humans, their mobile homes, and their wide variety of pets on my warship. I don't think I will ever understand the ones they call clowns. They are downright scary!" Manota admitted quietly. "You will see when you get home. Father has set them up not far outside of the city. He felt it would be better for them to slowly assimilate into our society so they do not cause a panic among our people. When will you be home?"

"In a few days," Jazin answered as he leaned back and ran his hands through his hair. "You know Tai Tek has disappeared again, don't you?"

"Yes," Manota growled out before he smiled cruelly. "But he is in for a surprise. I have located another stash of his credits. Not only that, he has made another enemy. Risteard Roald is not happy at being used. He has sent some of his own men after Tai Tek. The star systems have just gotten a little smaller. Even the mercenaries he has hired will not want to cross Risteard. The Grand Ruler is not known as a forgiving man."

Jazin let out a deep breath. The one good thing about Tai Tek's treachery was the alliance between Kassis and Elpidios. That star system had never welcomed others before. Now, they could build upon a mutual need and perhaps bring another star system into the Alliance. Having the Elpidios as an allied would strengthen the Alliance even more and provide more protection to travelers.

Gods, he was tired. He couldn't remember the last time he had slept. "Keep me posted of any changes," Jazin said leaning forward again. "We'll be home soon."

Manota laughed uneasily. "You will see what I mean when you get here," he said as he rubbed the back of his neck. "There is one human male I may have to kill. If I do, things might get bad. I'll tell you more about it later. Get some rest, brother. We are not as young as we used to be."

Jazin laughed and nodded. "I am feeling it. Until we meet again brother, be safe." Jazin signed off and stood up. It was time to go hold his little mate.

* * *

Star curled as close as she could get against Jazin's long form. Running her hand over his chest, she marveled that she had found someone so perfect for her. He had been so exhausted when he finally made it to their living quarters, she was amazed he could even walk.

She had wrapped her arm around him, murmuring tenderly to him to let her take care of him for once. His grumbling drew a chuckle from her, but he didn't resist as she guided him into the bathroom and tenderly washed the sweat and grime from his exhausted body. He had practically been asleep standing up by the time she finished. She seriously doubted he even remembered her drying him or helping him into the bed. He was asleep before his head even hit the pillow.

That had been almost fifteen hours ago. The only reason she had woken was because Armet had become worried and come to check on them. She had risen when she heard the request at the door two hours ago. After assuring Armet that Jazin was fine, just catching up on some desperately needed rest, she had used the restroom before crawling back in bed with him.

"I want to give you my child," Jazin's deep voice murmured softly into the dim light of their room. "Will you let me?"

Star's heart started in surprise. She had always dreamed of being a mother one day, but that was all it had ever been, a dream. She felt a shiver of need and desire sweep through her as his calloused palm feathered over her flat stomach.

"I want to see you rounded with our child," his voice thickened and deepened as his hand moved lower to cover the soft curls of her mound. "Will you let me give you my seed?" He groaned out as he rolled over to cage her under him.

Star looked up into his dark eyes. The silver highlights flaming with love and passion. Star smiled up at the beautiful face above her. Her hands moved up his side scraping his skin lightly with her fingernails before she wrapped them tightly around his neck.

"Yes," she whispered, pulling his head down. "Yes."

Jazin's fierce groan sounded loudly in the quiet room. His body reacted to the simple word. He ran his hand down along her hip before dipping into her hot channel to see if she was ready for him. He was more than ready for her. It was as if she ignited a torch inside of him with just a look, a touch, a scent of her delicate skin.

His fingers trembled as he tested her slick core. He reached between them and aligned his throbbing cock against her hot core. His eyes closed briefly at her heated gasp in his ear before he gripped her hip and pushed forward, ruthlessly stretching her as his control began to slip.

"Star," he gasped out as he embedded his cock to the hilt, the tip brushing up against her womb.

"Take me," she whispered back. "Forever, Jazin."

Jazin crushed his lips to hers as he began to rock harder and faster. He would take her over and over. His control disappearing as the fear of almost losing her and the adrenaline of battle broke loose.

His arms tightened around her to the point he knew he must be crushing her, but he couldn't seem to stop himself. He pushed deeper and harder as the tingling in his spine built and exploded outward. His loud cry echoed as he strained above her. He could feel her explode around his cock as he pulsed his seed deep into her. The feel of her milking him pulled another hoarse moan from him as her vaginal muscles gripped his cock, massaging it and pulling even more of his essence into her.

Their heavy pants were the only sound in the room for several minutes. Jazin ran his lips up and down along Star's neck sending shivers up and down her body in reaction to his tongue and teeth nipping her. The scent of her arousal combined with his was an aphrodisiac.

"Again," he grunted out.

"Again?" Star asked, dazed. "Are you serious?" She felt like she didn't have a solid bone in her body.

Jazin's eyes blazed and a wicked grin curved his lips. "I am well rested now. Again."

Star giggled and shook her head. "Well Mr. Well-rested, I need a shower."

Jazin's eyelids lowered and the grin on his face turned even more wicked if that was possible. "Good idea."

Star should have known she was in trouble from the grin on his face. Her startled squeal drew a chuckle from Jazin as he pulled out of her body and scooped her up into his arms rising from the bed in one fluid motion. She gripped his shoulder as her head spun from the rapid movement. Jazin called out the command to start the cleansing unit and stepped into it with her still in his arms.

He set her down long enough to reach out and snag a drying cloth. Star watched in confusion as he ripped it into strips. She sputtered when he grabbed her wrists and tied them together. Above the shower unit was a bar that could be used to hold onto if necessary. He flipped one end over it before he tied it around her wrists again. With a pull, he lifted her up off her feet until she was hanging in front of him. The only choice she had was to either hang from the bar or wrap her legs around his waist or over his shoulders.

She bit her lip before she lifted her leg up and put one slender thigh on each shoulder. This move opened her up to him, thrusting her hips forward and tilting her breasts upward. The deep growl of approval told her she had made the right choice.

"Now what?" She asked looking down at the dark head of her mate.

"Now this," he said, opening her to him.

Star's choked scream and the tightening of her thighs around his shoulders told him she liked him attacking her clit with his rough tongue. He licked, sucked, and nipped at it until she was struggling and begging him to give her release. Every time she would get close, he would pause or bite down on her clitoris until she was still again. He would train her to come on his command.

"I want you," she wailed out when he built her to exploding again then denied her.

"Only when I tell you," he growled out in satisfaction as the warm water washed down on them like the soft rains back home. "Tell me who you belong to," he purred against her as he slid two of his fingers deeply into her.

Star pulled up on her arms and looked down into Jazin's eyes as he stroked her slowly in and out. She fought to keep her eyes open as the tightening inside her body built again. "You, only you."

"Come for me," he responded as he pushed deeply into her at the same time as he clamped down on her swollen nub again with a mercilessness that pulled a shattered scream for her as her body exploded at the fierce attack.

Jazin never released her gaze as he drank the sweet crème pouring from her like a river suddenly escaping from the dam that had held it back for too long. He pulled back, sliding her legs from his shoulders. Rising, he turned her until she was facing away from him. He pulled her back and pushed through her swollen, over-sensitive lips until he was buried as deeply as he could go. He pulled on her distended nipples even as she fought against the invasion. Her body was on overload from his careful manipulations. He wanted to love her until she was mindless. He had succeeded.

She was mumbling wildly as he took her ruthlessly, pouring his seed into her again and again until he felt the moment her body opened to his and accepted it. He bent forward, biting down on her shoulder as she sobbed out begging him to let her come again. As his cock expanded and his hot seed poured into her, he pulled back enough to tell her to give him everything inside her. Those heated words of need washed through them both as her body responded to his in complete surrender.

Jazin held onto Star's limp body. He was still too hard to withdraw from her yet. A part of him knew he should be ashamed over what he had done, but he refused to feel any remorse. He was being selfish. He didn't want to take any chances of something trying to take his mate from him.

If they returned to his world and her parents tried to influence her feelings for him or there was another male from her past who wanted to stake a claim it would be a moot point. She would only respond to his body now. Not only that, she carried the heir to the House of Kassis. As such, she could never be taken from him except by death. He had sealed her to him completely, forever as she had asked.

He reached up and untied the strips of cloth he had used to tie her with. Giving the command, he switched the heated moisture of the shower to the soft, warmth of air that dried their bodies. He carefully pulled free of her body when he had softened enough to do so without causing either of them pain. Even so, he was still semi-hard. That appeared to be a constant state for him ever since the little warrior had come into his life.

He turned her gently in his arms, pressing her head against his shoulder as he stepped out of the cleansing unit. He carried her into their living quarters and laid her gently down on the bed. Reaching down, he tenderly brushed her hair away from her still flushed face. He waited patiently until her eyelashes fluttered before her eyes slowly opened. He raised the hand he clutched in his large hand to his mouth and pressed a kiss to her knuckles.

"Wow!" She said with a husky, shy laugh.

Jazin chuckled. "Wow."

"If I didn't get pregnant from that we are definitely going to have to try again," she muttered as she rose up into a sitting position and put a hand to her head as it spun. "That was…. Wow!"

Jazin's chuckle turned into a deep, satisfied laugh. He leaned forward and brushed a kiss along her full lips. "Your body accepted my seed. Soon you will grow round with our child. But, that does not mean we cannot continue practicing for the next time."

Star's hand dropped to her stomach at the same time her mouth dropped open. "How can you know whether I got pregnant or not? It will be weeks before we know."

Jazin shook his head. "No. I felt the moment your body opened and accepted my seed. A Kassisan warrior does not give his seed lightly and when he does, he knows when it is accepted. Soon, you will know I speak the truth. Your parents will have to accept me. You are mine forever, Star."

Star saw the vulnerability flash through Jazin's eyes as he mentioned her parents. A light clicked on as she thought about what had just happened. Her big, strong warrior was afraid. He was afraid of losing her. He was afraid of her parents not accepting him. He had absolutely nothing to fear.

"My parents are going to love you," she murmured. "You'll see. You are the man I love, forever," she reassured him tenderly.

She ran her fingers over the faint scar on his cheek that he received when they first met. That seemed like another lifetime ago. Her life back on Earth seemed surreal compared to her life now. She never thought she would be thankful for being kidnapped by a group of rebel aliens, but she would be forever thankful to the fate that set her destiny in motion.

Jazin's comlink sounded next to the bed and he released a sigh as he pulled back enough to reach over and activate it. "Speak."

"We are in orbit around Kassis. Crews from the planet have already started the resupply and transfer of the crew," Dakar stated.

"We will be ready shortly," Jazin said. "Tell Armet and Jarmen to prepare to depart with us. We need to meet with my father and brothers to discuss our next plan of offense against Tai Tek."

"Yes, my lord," Dakar responded.

Jazin released a deep breath as he turned to look at the relaxed features of his mate. His eyes roamed her nude figure and he bit back a groan as his body responded again. She was going to be the death of him.

"Come, let us get ready," he said. "I suspect your parents, sister, and River are anxious to see you."

Star's eyes lit up with delight. "Oh, I forgot all about them already! I can't think of anything else but you when I'm with you," she said with an excited giggle.

Jazin hid the smile of delight at her response as she moved to gather her clothes. He listened distractedly as they dressed. She told him about several members of her extended family. He could tell she had a deep affection for all of them as she shared story after story. Her tiny body practically hummed with suppressed energy as she moved.

He caught her in his arms just before they exited their living quarters. "I love you, Star Ja Kel Coradon."

A shy smile curved her lips as she pressed her lips against his briefly. "I love you too, Jazin Ja Kel Coradon. Don't you ever doubt it."

Chapter 21

Two weeks later, Jazin was watching in disbelief and with no small amount of fear as his mate flew through the air. His heart plummeted to his feet and didn't return to his chest until he saw her tiny hands grab the bar that was swung out to her. He was about to storm into the huge tent set up in the middle of the compound where Star's parents and the other species – humans – lived to get his tiny mate when two strange creatures with unusual white and black paint on their faces stopped him. They never said a word when he came. They just stopped him. There was something about them that always made him stop even if he didn't understand what it was. They didn't carry any weapons, they never touched him, but there was something that froze him in place as they acted like they had to search him, pulling outlandish things like scarves, feathers, even a strange furry thing with a long tail on it from his ear, the back of his vest, and other places. Then, they would act like there was an invisible door they had to unlock and open before he could enter. It was downright intimidating!

Personally, he agreed with his brother Manota about the clowns, but he could add a few other creatures as well. He moved through the invisible door trying to reach out his hand inconspicuously to see if he could feel anything as he went through. He even bent his head like the two figures taught him. He scowled deeply at them when they burst into fits of silent laughter at him.

One of these days I'm going to find out where in the Gods they found all those things on me, he thought as he shuddered when the hairy white creature with the long tail came into his mind and he rubbed his left ear where they had pulled it from.

He nodded at the two Frenchmen, Jon Paul and Luc, who were sitting further down near the bottom of the seats next to Madas and Gril. The two men were pointing out things to the two Tearnats as different members of the circus moved about doing different stunts. Jarmen had disappeared almost immediately when the two of them arrived without a word. He just shook his head at his friend's unusual behavior lately. He was more concerned with his own problems right now.

He climbed the metal seating that was set up and moved up to the center where Star's parents were sitting. He had to admit he liked Alan and Tami Strauss. They had accepted him warmly into their family. He had been introduced to many different species – humans – over the last two weeks. His eyes moved to the small man who was down near the center ring ordering people around and watched as they scrambled to do as he told them before turning back to the couple sitting contentedly watching everything.

"Good afternoon, Jazin," Tami Strauss said, rising up to give him a big hug and a kiss.

"Lady Tami," Jazin responded with an amused smile.

He was still unused to the affection of the humans. Star's mom was as tiny and petite as her daughter with the same white blond hair and light blue, twinkling eyes. Her father was several inches taller and had dark blond hair and dark blue eyes. He reached out and shook Jazin's hand before indicating he might as well sit for a while.

"Jazin," Alan Strauss nodded in greeting before he nodded toward where his two daughters were flying through the air. "They are beautiful to watch, aren't they?"

Jazin swallowed again as he watched Jo catch Star as she did a flip in the air. "Yes," he replied hoarsely. "I am not sure she should be doing this?"

Alan laughed as he watched Jazin's face pale a little. "You have to accept there is no stopping her. Tami was eight months pregnant with Jo and still flying through the air. Being a flyer is as much a part of us as the air we breathe."

Tami reached over and squeezed Jazin's hand in encouragement. "All Star has ever wanted was to be accepted for who and what she is. She may be small in stature but she is as tall as Jerry the Giant."

Jazin's eyes followed where a huge human male, almost eight feet tall, stood nodding at whatever the small ringmaster, Walter, was telling him. He watched as a young man walked in with several huge animals called horses.

The man swatted the one in the lead on its rump and it took off at a fast trot into the ring followed by the others. A few minutes later, his eyes rose to the top of the ring where two long ropes unfurled and Jo and Star worked their way down them. As the huge creatures passed under them, they dropped down lightly onto their backs.

A light film of sweat beaded his forehead as they both stood on the backs of the massive creatures as they circled the ring before jumping into the arms of a couple of clowns that came out of nowhere to catch them. The man who had brought the horses in whistled and the four creatures moved back out of the ring and through the tent exit on the far side.

"Walter is very, very strict about safety," Alan said, looking at Jazin with understanding. "He would never allow them to do anything that could harm them."

Jazin released a deep breath as he gave Tami and Alan a shaky smile. "I have never formally welcomed you to our world. Or formally asked for your daughter. In truth, I was not sure how you would react to your daughter mating with someone different from her."

Alan chuckled as he pulled his wife closer to him. "Look around you, Jazin. Star has been raised her whole life to accept those that are different. I won't say we were not a little worried and concerned when we first met Manota or saw the shuttles that ferried us up to the spaceship that carried us to this remarkable world," Alan began.

"Or when we heard that Star had been hurt," Tami added softly squeezing her husband's hand. "But, we have always hoped that our daughters would find someone who could make them happy, complete. I feel that you do that with Star."

Jazin saw the sincerity in their eyes. "I would give my life to protect your daughter. I love her deeply. She has proven to be a warrior in her own right. I would have died if not for her skills," Jazin admitted as he watched Star and Jo laughing with several people who had joined them down below.

"Is it true that your people believe that Jo, Star, and River are part of a prophesy?" Alan asked hesitantly. "Your brother mentioned it."

Jazin's head turned in surprise that Manota had shared this information so soon. He would have thought his brother would have held back, concerned that Jo and Star's parents would be reluctant to allow their daughters to mate with them knowing there was a possibility of danger to them.

He cleared his throat before he answered. "Yes, it is believed they were the three warriors mentioned in a prophecy from long ago. Their strength and skills will save and unite the House of Kassis. I have to believe it is true. River saved my brother, Torak, from an assassin. Star saved my life when I was kidnapped. Star….," Jazin paused as his gaze softened on his mate's glowing face. "Star had a vision. She saw us together in another lifetime. I am named after a great warrior from long ago. Our world had been attacked and our people were brought to the point of extinction from the invasion. On the night when the two moons of Kassis formed one, the stormy skies opened up and from the heavens, the Gods and

Goddesses rained down like rain destroying our enemies. One fighter descended to where my ancestor stood in fierce defiance. From the fighter, his mate, the Goddess Starla, appeared before him. He claimed her and together they built the House of Kassis, bringing hope and love to its people. Just as your daughter has brought hope and love to me."

Tami wiped a tear from her cheek and gave a small, embarrassed laugh. "Well, who are we to deny that!"

Alan pressed a kiss against his wife's temple. "Welcome to the family, son. I know you'll take good care of our little girl."

Jazin looked down and smiled before he looked at Alan and Tami with a resigned smile. "I think she will be taking just as good a care of me as I will her. I would like to invite you to our home for a dinner to welcome you to our world."

"We'll be honored to attend," Alan said. "Isn't that your father?"

Jazin looked down as his father and Risteárd Roald walked into the huge tent. They paused to talk with Walter, who came hurrying up to them when Risteárd raised a sword at the two painted-faced men who were always stopping him at the entrance. "Yes, he has been stopping by regularly to talk with Walter."

"Who is the other man?" Tami asked, eyeing the huge, blue-skinned man who was looking around the arena with narrowed eyes. "He looks a little scary. I wouldn't be surprised if Walter doesn't try to hire him."

Jazin's chuckle was rich and deep at the thought of Ristéard Roald, the Grand Ruler of Elpidios, being ordered around by the little human male. While he could appreciate the authority the small man obviously had over those in the circus, he highly doubted that the man would have a chance in hell of success at bossing the huge warrior around. Jazin's eyes widened when he heard a low, deep snarl erupt from Ristéard. His eyes followed where the Grand Ruler was looking and he chuckled. It looked like something had caught the big blue warrior's attention and he didn't like the idea of someone else having the same thoughts.

A tall, slender female wearing knee high black boots, a slim skirt that ended just above her knees, and a soft, blue long sleeved blouse was talking to the two men who had stopped him when he first came in. She glanced over at Ristéard with a dark frown on her face before turning her attention back to the men. He studied the female carefully.

She was very tall for a human female, over six feet if he was to make a guess. Her dark blond hair was pulled back into a tight bun at the back of her head and she was wearing something over her eyes. She was lovely in a long, gangly way. She reminded him of the slender animals that gazed in the forests near his mountain retreat.

He heard Walter yell out something and the female turned with the frown still on her face. "Who is that?" He asked curiously.

"That's Walter and Nema's daughter, Ricki. She handles all the travel, legal, and business issues for the circus. She is the glue that keeps everything together. She is very thorough and keeps everything running smoothly in the background," Tami responded.

Jazin looked from Walter's small figure to that of the female who was walking toward him. He had also remembered that Walter's mate was even smaller than he was. How was it possible for them to....

"They adopted Ricki when she was an infant," Alan explained seeing Jazin's confused expression. "She was left on the steps of their trailer. A brief note begging them to care for the baby."

"Nema couldn't have children and Ricki was a blessing to them," Tami said as she watched Ricki listen carefully to what her father was telling her. Tami gasped suddenly as the huge blue man took a menacing step toward the shy girl.

"He will not harm her," Jazin assured Tami and Alan. "My father would not allow it."

Alan chuckled as they watched Walter turn on the huge warrior with a deep scowl and lit into him as Ricki turned on her heel and left the tent quickly. Jazin wasn't sure what was being said, but the look on Risteárd's face was enough to let him know that the Grand Ruler was not happy. The Grand Ruler's eyes didn't return to Walter until the female could no longer be seen.

"Hi!" Star said, stepping in front of him, blocking his view of the Grand Ruler, his father, and Walter.

He looked up startled and grinned before he realized what he was doing. He was a warrior and here he was grinning like a young boy with his first female. He reached out and grabbed his mate and pulled her down onto his lap, kissing her passionately right there in front of her parents, those crazy clowns, his father, the Grand Ruler, and the Gods and Goddesses.

Who the hell cares if he had a grin as goofy as those two Frenchmen they had rescued, or as stupid as a young lad, he thought as she returned his heated kiss. *He was just fitting in with the rest of the strange and unusual characters his brother had brought back.*

He ignored the sighs next to him and the loud whistles filling the huge tent as he pressed his claim. His life had changed so much since a tiny warrior from another world entered his life and he wouldn't change a single, solitary thing about it. Clowns, drunk Frenchmen, an adventuresome Tearnat female, or the other two beautiful warriors who helped corrupt the one in his arms every chance they got.

No, I don't care one iota, he thought as he lost himself to the storm his amazing little warrior from another world stirred up inside him.

To be continued…. **Jo's Journey**

Star's Storm~ 271 ~

Preview of _Jo's Journey_

(Lords of Kassis: Book 3)

Synopsis

Jo Strauss was committed to two things in her life – her family and her life as an acrobat/high-wire performer. She takes both very seriously. Her life was orderly, in control, and she was finally settling down in one place so she could spend more time with her parents instead of moving all over the world every few weeks. To celebrate her and younger sister Star's one year anniversary away from the circus they had grown up with, she and Star were meeting River Knight, their childhood friend and sister of the heart, for a vacation in the mountains in North Carolina.

Everything goes as planned until she and her sisters are kidnapped. Now, she finds herself transported to another world. Aliens, warships, battles and a certain male were not in the carefully detailed plans she had mapped out for her life.

Manota Ja Kel Coradon is the second son of the ruling House of Kassis. He is known as the dark brother, a reputation that he lives up to. He has fought hard to protect his family and the people of Kassis, at times sacrificing parts of his soul to do so. His knowledge, skills and development of weaponry are legendary. His skill as a warrior bring shivers of fear to his opponents who know he never gives mercy to any who stand in his way.

Manota is in total control of his world until one slender, feisty alien female crashes through the shields he has placed around his heart. She is fearless, determined and stubborn. She absolutely refuses to cower before him, no matter how much he growls! He is determined to protect her and claim her as his own but there is one little problem – she will not agree to accept his claim unless he returns for her parents.

Now, he has even bigger problems – that come in all different shapes, sizes and species! The return trip is fraught with enough dangers, but Jo and Star's parents aren't the only ones coming back to Kassis - so is the circus family who had gathered to help look for their missing family members.

Traitors, pirates and Mimes are just the tip of the iceberg of trouble gliding through warp speed to his home world. Manota is about to learn that the prophecy that was foretold centuries before is true. His mate is just as much of a warrior as he is and she comes with backup when an old enemy attacks!

If you loved this story by me (S.E. Smith) please leave a review. You can also take a look at additional books and sign up for my newsletter at **http://sesmithfl.com** to hear about my latest releases or keep in touch using the following links:

Website: http://sesmithfl.com
Newsletter: http://sesmithfl.com/?s=newsletter
Facebook: https://www.facebook.com/se.smith.5
Twitter: https://twitter.com/sesmithfl
Pinterest: http://www.pinterest.com/sesmithfl/
Blog: http://sesmithfl.com/blog/
Forum: http://www.sesmithromance.com/forum/

Excerpts of S.E. Smith Books

If you would like to read more S.E. Smith stories, she recommends Hunter's Claim, the first in her Alliance series. Or if you prefer a Paranormal or Western with a twist, you can check out Lily's Cowboys or Indiana Wild…

Additional Books by S.E. Smith

Short Stories and Novellas
For the Love of Tia
    (Dragon Lords of Valdier Book 4.1)
A Dragonling's Easter
    (Dragonlings of Valdier Book 1.1)
A Dragonling's Haunted Halloween
    (Dragonlings of Valdier Book 1.2)

Viper's Defiant Mate (Sarafin Warriors Book 2)
The Alliance Series
Hunter's Claim (The Alliance: Book 1)
Razor's Traitorous Heart (The Alliance: Book 2)
Dagger's Hope (The Alliance: Book 3)
Zion Warriors Series
Gracie's Touch (Zion Warriors: Book 1)
Krac's Firebrand (Zion Warriors: Book 2)

Paranormal and Time Travel Novels
Spirit Pass Series
Indiana Wild (Spirit Pass: Book 1)
Spirit Warrior (Spirit Pass Book 2)
Second Chance Series
Lily's Cowboys (Second Chance: Book 1)
Touching Rune (Second Chance: Book 2)

Young Adult Novels
Breaking Free Series
Voyage of the Defiance (Breaking Free: Book 1)

Recommended Reading Order Lists:
http://sesmithfl.com/reading-list-by-events/
http://sesmithfl.com/reading-list-by-series/

About S.E. Smith

S.E. Smith is a *New York Times*, *USA TODAY*, *International, and Award-Winning* Bestselling author of science fiction, fantasy, paranormal, and contemporary works for adults, young adults, and children. She enjoys writing a wide variety of genres that pull her readers into worlds that take them away.

CPSIA information can be obtained
at www.ICGtesting.com
Printed in the USA
BVHW091411041118
532125BV00012B/300/P